Snow Foal

For my precious mum, Jean,
who really could paint light
on water.

Snow Foal

SUSANNA BAILEY

EGMONT

EGMONT
We bring stories to life

First published in Great Britain in 2019
by Egmont UK Limited
2 Minster Court, 10th Floor, London, EC3R 7BB

Text copyright © 2019 Susanna Bailey

ISBN 978 1 4052 94935

A CIP catalogue record for this title
is available from the British Library

70521/4

Printed and bound in Great Britain by CPI Group
Typeset by Avon DataSet Ltd, Bidford on Avon, Warwickshire

MIX
Paper from
responsible sources
FSC® C020471

PROLOGUE

Everything around him was changed: white, shifting, silent. The wind had form now: it swirled around him, like feathers from the forest floor, hiding the sky. Hiding his mother.

The foal sniffed the ground. That had changed, too. It clung to his muzzle. It stung.

He smelled the air, seeking his mother's warm, milky scent. He called. Listened. Called again. He thought he heard his mother's voice lifting through the trees.

His mother was gone.

Driven by hunger, the foal left the shelter of the old oaks, and drifted across the open moor. He nuzzled the newly white earth, seeking green blades of grass, or the prickly yellow gorse he had been learning to eat alongside his mother's milk.

He moved slowly, his body tensed for flight. He listened out for the black monster, with its glaring eyes and thunderous roar.

And for the humans who had forced his mother into its terrible jaws.

As darkness fell, and the moon spilled silver light across the moorland, instinct pulled the foal towards the protection of the hedgerow. He pushed his soft muzzle beneath frozen branches, twisted his tongue around the bitter, brittle leaves that nestled beneath. He shook snow from his nostrils and stretched forward, searching for more food.

Then he was sliding, falling: thin legs flailing amidst a tangle of sharp twigs. Snow slid with him, pressing him into the ditch behind the hedge.

When he opened his eyes, the foal could no longer find the moon.

ONE

Addie couldn't see much at all now that they'd left the town, with its pale streetlamps, and vivid neon signs. Just glimpses of flat fields and shadowy forests; of spiked hedges and trees edged with white, wavering like ghosts in the beam from the car headlights.

'Not much further,' Penny said. She glanced over her shoulder at Addie. 'We should see the farmhouse soon.' She squinted out through the windscreen again, adjusted her round glasses. 'This weather's slowed us up a bit. You must be so tired.'

Addie shrugged, watched the wipers whip back and forth through the sleet and snow. Penny's car struggled on, taking her further and further away from her brown brick home.

Further away from Mam.

They hadn't let Addie go in the ambulance with Mam. They'd made tea with too much sugar; made Addie sit down in the wrong chair in the lounge. Addie hated them. Hated their radios that crackled and hissed, their silver buttons that flashed in the light. Their eyes that swept the room and decided things.

'Penny, can we ring Mam when we get there?' Addie asked. 'Tell her I'll be back in the morning?'

'It's late, Addie. Your mum needs to rest, sweetheart. I'll check on her first thing. And then I'll come and talk to you. I promise.' Penny slowed the car, turned it to the left. Her long nails flashed red on the steering wheel.

'I can't stay here tomorrow,' Addie said. 'Mam'll worry.'

Penny sighed. A soft, sad sound. Was she even listening?

The car bumped along a rough track. Addie's stomach lurched. She chewed at the skin around her thumb nail. Where were they?

A white light cut through the darkness, revealed a wooden sign on a tall pole. Penny leaned forward, slowed the car down. 'There we are,' she said. 'They've left the gate open for us. We're here.'

❄

TWO

The farmhouse was huge: the biggest house Addie had ever seen. Wide windows threw yellow light on to a snow-covered courtyard. Smoke curled from tall chimneys into the night.

The door opened as Addie and Penny approached, and a small woman in Wellington boots hurried across the yard to meet them. She was holding a jacket round her shoulders. Addie saw that she was wearing pyjamas underneath

'You made it,' she said. 'I was worried. The weather's really closed in since this morning.'

'Hi, Ruth,' said Penny. 'Sorry it's got so late. These roads . . .'

'Not to worry. You're here now, that's the main thing.' Ruth smiled at Addie. 'Let's get you both inside.' She hurried them through the door into a long, bright hallway full of jackets, boots and bags. 'Come on into the kitchen. And let me have your

5

coats,' she said, 'I'll put them by the fire to dry.'

The fire in the kitchen was a real one inside a huge, brick hearth. 'Get it going a bit more, shall we, Addie?' Ruth said, smiling again. She pointed to a wooden rocking chair by the hearth. 'Sit here, when you're done, love. Warm yourself. But pop those trainers off first, I would. They look soaked.' She bent down and poked at the fire with some kind of stick. Small red flames licked up around the logs inside.

Addie watched them for a moment. She could smell smoke. It made her throat tickle.

She stayed where she was, folded her arms across her chest.

'When you're ready then,' Ruth said. 'You take your time.' She moved across to the table and lifted foil from a large plate 'I've made some sandwiches for you both.' She turned back to Addie, smiled again. 'And there's hot chocolate too. I expect you'd like some of that, Addie? Penny, how about you?'

'Perfect,' Penny said. She put her briefcase on the table. Addie stared at it. She knew all about that briefcase, with its files full of secrets and lies.

She looked away.

She was freezing cold, even in Ruth's warm

kitchen. Her toes felt as if something was biting them. And she *was* thirsty. 'Yes,' she said to Ruth. 'Hot chocolate. Please.'

Ruth smiled still more broadly. 'Good,' she said. 'Won't be a mo.' She moved a shiny copper pan from the bench on to the stove and began to stir it.

Addie stared down at her feet. Snow slid from her shoes on to the tiled floor and quickly melted there. She glanced up. Had Ruth noticed?

She hadn't. She was deep in conversation with Penny, over by the stove.

Addie pulled at her wet laces, took off her trainers. She held them up for a moment. Where was she supposed to put them? Nobody had said. She pushed them out of sight, under her chair, clutched her damp coat collar closer round her neck. She looked around.

It was the kind of kitchen you see in films, or in magazines at the doctor's surgery. Big tiles on the floor, big wooden furniture, big dark beams across the ceiling. There was an enormous fridge covered in stickers, scribbled notes and photographs of children. Addie wondered who the children were and whether they all lived here, with Ruth and Sam.

Whatever Penny and Ruth were planning, Addie's photo was never going on that fridge.

She strained to hear what Penny was saying to Ruth. Penny had her serious face on, which was worrying. Ruth was nodding. She glanced over at Addie, her eyes soft and watery. Like the police officer's eyes, just before she made Addie let go of Mam's hand.

'Almost done, Addie,' she said, smiling. She turned back to the stove, stirred her pan of milk, as if everything was normal. As if everything was fine.

Ruth didn't look like a foster carer. Not like Dawn anyway. Dawn, with her pink hair and high heels, her endless phone calls, her high-pitched laugh. Dawn, who hardly spoke to Addie for the whole weekend she spent there in the summer. Dawn, who never smiled.

Ruth's face looked as if it was used to smiling. Her brown hair was scooped into a kind of nest on the top of her head. It bobbed from side to side as she moved around the kitchen, quick as bird. And she still had her boots on. Dawn would bust a gut. It was shoes off at the door in her house.

Ruth would have rules, too, Addie thought – rules for children like her, who didn't really belong in this house. She would tell Addie what they were when Penny had gone. Like Dawn did.

Ruth reached over Addie's shoulder; put a tray of drinks and a plate of thick, brown sandwiches on the table. 'Help yourself, love,' she said. 'Just say if you want more.'

'I'm not hungry,' Addie said. She watched as Penny took a sandwich, bit into it, chewed. A piece of tomato dropped on to her chest and rested on her multi-coloured beads.

'What time are you coming back, Penny? In the morning?' Addie asked.

Penny looked over at Ruth, swallowed her mouthful of food. 'As early as I can, Addie,' she said. 'Once I've had a chance to find out what the plan is with your mum.' She took another bite of sandwich, held the remainder in the air. There was pink lipstick on the edge of the bread.

'She'll be fine tomorrow,' Addie said. She looked at Ruth. 'She just needed more sleep, that's all.'

'Why don't we let you get some sleep as well,' said Ruth said. 'If you're sure you don't need to eat. I was hoping you might be able to meet the boys before bed, but they're still out checking the fields. This weather

9

closed in really quickly and we have to bring the sheep in closer to the farm. There're a few stragglers still out there. She pointed to the sandwiches, laughed again. 'They'll make short work of your leftovers when they do get back, Addie.'

Addie stared at her. She didn't care about sheep and she didn't care about Ruth's family. All she cared about was making the morning come as quickly as possible. 'Come and see your room then,' Ruth said. She sat down, pulled off her boots. 'Bring your drink if you like.' She gave Addie another of her smiles. 'There's someone rather special waiting to meet you upstairs.'

'I just want to go to sleep,' Addie said. She gulped down her hot drink, wiped her hand across her mouth, got to her feet.

'Best thing,' said Penny. 'Try not to worry, love. Your mum's in the right place just now.'

Addie bit her lip. Why did adults always say that when they knew it wasn't true? She turned her back on Penny and followed Ruth to the door.

'Goodnight, Addie,' Penny called. 'See you very soon.'

Addie looked over her shoulder. Penny was taking papers from her bag: papers about Addie. Papers for deciding things.

Papers for keeping her away from Mam.

'It's all my fault,' she said. 'Just stupid, stupid me. Write that on your stupid papers.'

❄ ❄ ❄

Addie peered out through splinters of frost on the hall window. Early light now. No one about except Mrs Donovan, shuffling up her drive with her bags.

Perhaps they weren't coming, after all.

Could Addie risk going out? Was that a stupid idea?

She had to go. She was starving. And Mam would need something when she woke.

She stood on the doorstep, pulled up her hood. Her breath floated on the air for a moment, then disappeared. She counted the coins again: just enough, with the fifty pence from under the fridge. She checked up and down the grey street. Nobody at all now. Just cracked puddles and litter drifting in the gutter; the still, orange light from the corner shop.

Addie hurried past the squashed row of brown brick houses with their faded doors and broken fences. She stayed close to the kerb, kept her head down. The baby at number six was screaming again. A dog started to bark.

Addie pushed open the shop door. The bell clanged. She peered round the shelves. Please let it be Mr Borovski today, she thought. Not Mrs Crabtree, with her thin nose poking into everyone's business. Mrs Crabtree who noticed things.

No such luck. Mrs Crabtree came out from behind the counter and folded her arms across her bony chest. She watched Addie's every move, looked her up and down; hovered like a hungry crow.

Addie thumped the brown loaf and milk down by the till. 'One pound, ten pence,' she said. 'The bread's reduced.' She pointed to the yellow sticker and counted the coins into Mrs Crabtree's hand.

The shopkeeper poked at them with a thin finger, pulled a piece of dark fluff from among them. 'I've not seen your mam in a while,' she said. 'Under the weather again, is she?'

Addie grabbed her shopping. 'She's busy, that's all,' she said. 'With her painting.' She turned away, felt the burn of Mrs Crabtree's eyes as she hurried from the shop.

THREE

Sunni did look quite special. She had hair like dark glass and black lines painted around her eyes. And she was tiny. Even though Ruth said she was only a year younger than Addie.

'Your bed's that one,' Sunni said, pointing to a wooden bed in the corner. Addie's purple duvet from home was on it and her best pyjamas were laid out ready. They didn't look right in this room. Someone had put a blue dressing gown there too. It wasn't hers.

'I know everything's strange for you, sweetheart,' Ruth said, 'but you must be so tired after today. You and Sunni get to know one another a bit. I'll pop down for hot-water bottles. Then we'll get you girls settled. OK?'

It wasn't OK. Nothing was. But Addie nodded.

'You can put your things on the bottom shelf,' Sunni said. 'The top one's mine. But don't touch my stuff unless you ask me first, OK?' She cocked her head to one side and Addie saw the sparkle of a gold earring under her hair.

'I'm going home soon,' Addie said. 'I don't need a shelf.'

13

'Ruth and Sam only foster kids who have to stay a long time,' Sunni said. 'Like me.'

'Well, I'm not staying for long. Mam won't let me.'

Sunni shrugged her shoulders. 'My mum wants me to come home too, only she couldn't learn how to look after me properly, so I'm staying here.'

'Forever?' Addie said.

'Expect so.'

'Don't you mind?'

Sunni was searching through a collection of bright ornaments on her shelf. 'Sort of, but I like it here. They've got chickens and pigs and I get to feed them. It's cool. And there's this really grumpy goat called Jelly. He got his name cos his favourite thing in the whole world is Jelly Babies. What do you think of that?'

Addie had never known anyone who kept pigs, chickens *or* goats. And she'd never heard of a goat eating Jelly Babies. She thought of the night-time foxes that raided the bins in her street. She'd seen one of them devouring a bag of popcorn, warning others to keep away with a slant-eyed stare. She didn't say so. She didn't think Sunni would be impressed.

Sunni held up a sequinned elephant. 'This is my mum's. She gave me it the last time I saw her.'

'I've got this,' Addie said. She brought a curled pink and white shell from her pocket, held it in the palm of her hand. 'Mam's lucky shell. It's from Whitby, near where she grew up.'

Sunni picked it up and held it up to one eye. 'Something used to live in here,' she said. 'It must be dead now.' She tossed the shell back to Addie. Like it was nothing. 'What's happened to your mum, then?'

'Nothing's happened to her. She's not feeling very well, that's all.'

'What kind of "not very well"?' Sunni inspected Addie's pyjamas. 'Is she dying?'

'No, she's not! And don't touch my things either.' Addie snatched her pyjama jacket back from Sunni.

'I don't like pyjamas,' Sunni said. 'I like nightdresses. This is my favourite.' She twirled round twice to show if off. It was blue and green, like peacock feathers.

'Mam and me like pyjamas,' Addie said. 'We don't wear dresses.'

Sunni pulled a face and flung herself down on her bed. 'Where's your dad, then?' she said.

'Haven't got one.'

'Everyone's got one. Didn't your mum tell you who yours is?'

'Course she did,' Addie said.

'Right, Sunni,' Ruth said, bustling back into the room. 'Time to let Addie get some sleep.' She gave Addie a purple hot-water bottle with a furry cover.

'Do you think you can settle off to sleep, Addie?' asked Ruth. 'Or would you like to read for a bit?'

Addie shook her head. At home she liked to read in bed; liked to disappear for a while among the pages. Sometimes, she became small again, curled next to Mam, following her finger across the strange black shapes that held the stories. Sometimes, she became someone brave and strong. Someone who knew how to fix things.

Sometimes, reading helped.

It wouldn't help tonight. Nothing would.

Addie just wanted Ruth to go away.

By the time Addie had undressed and cleaned her teeth in the bathroom, Sunni was in bed. She didn't look up from her book when Addie came into the room. Addie was glad. She crawled under her duvet, pulling it right up over her head. It smelled of home. She pressed her eyes shut and pretended she was back there in her own bed. She was small. Really small. The door was open and Mam was asleep in the next room.

❋ ❋ ❋

The dream woke Addie, as it always did.

For a moment, she didn't know where she was. Her heart hammered in her ears; her hair was sticky on her forehead. She felt sick.

She took a deep breath, like her mam had told her. It only helped a bit.

The bedroom was so dark. The deepest dark Addie had ever seen. It was full of silence. Full of nothing.

At home there was a streetlamp outside Addie's bedroom window. It shone through her curtains like a small yellow sun. It kept her company when she couldn't sleep. At home, it was never quiet. Even at night. There was always the hum of traffic, the slamming of doors, the call of cats.

At home, there was always Mam.

Mam didn't like the night. She wandered around the house until morning. She needed her loud music and her drinks to get her through the dark space in between. She needed Addie.

Who was looking after Mam tonight?

Addie curled up under her duvet, wrapped her arms tightly round herself. She tried to make out Sunni's bed on the opposite side of the room. She listened for her breathing, could just make out its soft rhythm; the occasional gentle snore.

Her eyes became heavy as she lay listening. If she went to sleep again, she wouldn't have the bad feeling in her stomach. But the dream might come again. She needed to stay awake.

An owl hooted. Once. Twice. Something screeched. Something near the house. Addie shivered in her duvet nest. She lay very still.

Everything was quiet again.

She was thirsty now. Could she get a drink from the bathroom? She might wake Sunni if she got up. Or Ruth. Or Sam. She didn't think Ruth would mind, but what about Sam? He'd been out working until late, Ruth said. He'd be very tired. People got angry when they were tired.

Addie would have to wait.

She stared at the window. How long was it until morning?

FOUR

Addie crawled to the end of her bed and pulled one of the curtains aside. She leaned a hand against the windowpane, tried to see outside. It left its shape there when she moved, a ghost hand among stars of frost on the cold glass.

It wasn't really morning yet. Just fingers of pale light in the yard below. But Addie could see that more snow had fallen overnight. Much more. Not the sleety mess that fell in the town, slippery and slimy in the streets, grey and dirty in the gutters. Proper snow. Snow you could build things with. Perfect snow, glistening silvery white as far as Addie could see: like the snow in the paintings Mam did. Before.

Would the snow stop Penny coming back for her? Ruth had said something about the difficult roads near the farm. Addie closed the curtain again and got down from her bed. Pretty as it was, it had better stop falling soon.

She found yesterday's jeans and jumper on the chair by her bed, and put them on over her pyjamas. She tiptoed past Sunni's bed, the wooden floor smooth and cold under her bare feet.

One of the floorboards near the door creaked as Addie stepped on it. Sunni stirred, flung one arm out of her covers and over the edge of the bed. There was a gentle clinking sound. Addie stood still. She held her breath. She waited. Watched. Something sparkled on Sunni's wrist: she was still wearing her bracelets.

Sunni didn't move again, so Addie edged out of the room and along the dim landing in the direction she remembered the bathroom to be. Her heart pounded as she passed two closed doors on her right-hand side. Which was Ruth and Sam's room? Addie couldn't remember.

Would they mind that she was up?

The door next to the bathroom was partly open, blue light spilling from inside on to the floor in front of Addie. The bathroom was on the other side of it, so Addie would have to go past to get a drink. She glanced inside the room as she did so, fingers crossed behind her back. A small child was sitting bolt upright in bed, pale hair gleaming like a halo in the watery blue light. He or

20

she, Addie couldn't tell, was staring straight at her.

Addie stared back as she passed, willing whoever it was to keep quiet. They did.

There was a stack of coloured plastic cups by the bathroom sink. Addie filled a green one with water from the tap. It tasted different from the water at home. Cleaner. Nicer. She drained the cup, filled it again. She could take it back to her room.

When she passed the open door again, the child was huddled under the bedclothes. Addie heard soft, thin sounds, like a kitten crying for its mother.

Sunni had switched on the light and was sitting up in bed, brushing her hair. She gave Addie a small, quick smile. Perhaps she didn't mind that Addie had woken her. Addie tried to smile back, but her mouth felt stiff. Should she tell Sunni about the child? Would whoever it was want anyone to know they were upset? Maybe not. She drank her water, wondered what to do next.

A door slammed downstairs. Somebody whistled in the yard outside the window. Someone else was up then.

'That's Gabe,' Sunni said, straightening her bed covers. 'And Flo. They're off to see to the cows.'

Addie stared at her. 'In the dark?'

Sunni rolled her eyes, as if Addie had said something really stupid.

'Who's Gabe?' Addie said quickly.

'Ruth and Sam's son. He's fourteen. He's got a guitar and he lets me play it.' She looked at Addie, stared into her eyes. 'I'm the only one that's allowed.'

Addie turned away. She peeped out through the curtains again. She couldn't see anyone. She still couldn't see much at all, except the snow, and patches of orange light from two downstairs windows.

'Is Flo Gabe's sister, then?' she asked.

'She's a sheepdog,' said Sunni, shoving her feet into fleecy slippers. 'She goes everywhere with Gabe. She's a bit bonkers. Like him.' She pulled a scarlet dressing gown round her shoulders. She looked Addie up and down. 'We don't get dressed for breakfast,' she said. 'We go down in our nightclothes.'

'I don't,' said Addie. 'Except at home.'

'Well, this is a foster home. It's the same.'

Addie shook her head. 'It isn't. And anyway, my social worker's coming back this morning. Early. So I'm ready. And I'm not having breakfast.'

'She's not taking you home, if that's what you think,' Sunni said. 'And you have to have breakfast. That's the rule. Come on . . . before Jude eats all the toast.' Sunni flounced to the door, her dressing gown floating behind her like a cape. 'Oh, and that's Jude's cup you've got there,' she said over her shoulder. 'He'll go nuts.'

Was Jude the child in the other bedroom? Addie didn't like the sound of him. She put the green cup down on Sunni's shelf, among her collection of elephants. 'Wait a minute,' she shouted, 'I've got bare feet.'

But Sunni was gone.

Addie's feet were freezing. She looked around for the bag Penny had made her pack. Her favourite socks were in there. The rainbow ones Mam chose.

The bag was at the foot of the bed. It was empty. Where were her things?

'Addie, sweetheart. Good morning! I wondered if it was you I heard up and about just now.' Ruth was in the doorway, wiping her hands on her apron. Addie turned away, pretended to search in the front pocket of her bag.

Ruth perched on the end of Sunni's bed. 'I put your clean things in the drawers for you, love. The ones with the blue handles. Breakfast's ready, so pop something on your feet and we'll go down together, shall we?'

Addie's fists tightened. 'I like my things in my bag,' she said.

'That's OK, Addie. Put them back for now then. I understand.'

It wasn't OK. Nothing was. And Ruth didn't understand anything. Addie pulled on her trainers. She would do without socks.

And she would do without Ruth's breakfast. Whatever the stupid rule was.

FIVE

The fire was burning in the kitchen again. The room smelled of wood smoke and toast. The table had a red and white checked cloth on it this morning. In the middle was a basket of eggs, a plate piled high with toast and some boxes of cereal. Addie had never seen so much food.

Sunni was eating a bowl of Addie's favourite Cocoa Puffs. She waved her spoon at Addie. This time she didn't smile.

'Sit yourself down, Addie,' Ruth said. 'Do you like eggs?' She pointed to the basket. The eggs inside were brown and speckled. Not at all like the ones from Mr Borovski's shop, or the supermarket in the precinct. There was a tiny brown feather stuck to one of them.

'Freshly laid,' Ruth said. She smiled. 'I've got two of the biggest nearly ready, especially for you.'

'I'm not hungry,' Addie said. She didn't like this kitchen that pretended to be a happy place. And she didn't like Ruth pretending to be her mam.

'I'll make you a hot chocolate then, shall I? You might feel hungrier in a bit.' Ruth lifted a huge yellow jug from the table and took it to the stove

'That's goat's milk in that jug,' Sunni said. 'Bet you've never had that before.'

Addie hadn't, but she didn't say so. She pulled back a chair.

'Not there,' Sunni said. 'That's next to Jude's seat.'

'So?' said Addie.

'He doesn't let anyone sit next to him.'

'Why not?' said Addie. Jude sounded horrible.

'Just doesn't,' said Sunni, shrugging. She reached for a carton of orange juice and poured some for herself.

Ruth came across to the table and pulled out the chair next to Sunni. It had a blue cushion on it. A fat ginger cat was sleeping there.

'Sit here, Addie, love,' Ruth said. 'Widget, off.'

Widget opened one green eye. Then the other. He jumped down and stared at Addie, his tail twitching from side to side. Then he curled himself round Addie's legs and walked slowly away.

'He likes you,' Ruth said. 'He usually ignores new people at first.'

Addie sat down. Widget had left his warm smell behind him on her chair. She wished he would come back.

A small boy came into the kitchen. His wrists and ankles poked out from Superman pyjamas, thin as winter twigs. He stopped, peered at Addie from underneath pale curls, stared down at his feet.

The child with the blue light.

Addie watched him, noticed how he twisted his hands together; saw the shadows under his eyes.

'That's Jude,' Sunni said. 'He's six but he can't talk.'

Ruth handed Addie a mug of hot chocolate. 'Jude *can* talk, Sunni. Remember? He just doesn't feel like talking *to us* right now.'

She gave Jude a reassuring nod, brought him over to his chair. He knelt up on it and grabbed three slices of toast. Then he reached for Sunni's cereal packet.

'He eats loads,' said Sunni.

'Maybe we could save the cereal for later, Jude?' Ruth said, taking the box from him. 'We can keep it out on the side here, for when you need it.' She held out her hand. Jude clutched the box for a moment, then let go. He looked up at Addie. His eyes were huge, deep blue, and still as a lake. Addie smiled at him, but he looked away.

Ruth took the tops off two eggs for him and one for Addie. 'Just in case.'

Jude shoved spoonfuls of egg and huge chunks of toast into his mouth, all at the same time. He made slurping sounds as he ate. Addie tried not to look at him. She could tell he wouldn't want her to. She sipped her hot chocolate. It was warm and creamy, nicer than the one she'd tried the night before. But not as nice as the cocoa Mam made. When she remembered to buy milk.

Sunni kept talking non-stop, telling Ruth about her best friend from school, Mira, and her amazing house. Addie was glad. She didn't want to speak to either of them.

Ruth's phone rang.

'I need to take this,' Ruth said. 'I'll just be in the lounge. Won't be long.' As she passed Jude's chair, she rested her hand on his head for a moment; smiled over her shoulder at Addie.

As soon as she was gone, Jude got down from the table and took the cereal packet again.

'No, Jude,' Sunni said. 'Ruth wants you to leave it till later.'

Jude stuffed his hand inside the box. Sunni got down

28

from the table and snatched it from him. Pieces of chocolate rice flew into the air and skidded across the floor. Jude's face turned bright red. He screamed: a thin, wild scream. Like the creature in the night. It made Addie's heart hurt.

Ruth came running in. She sent Sunni off to get ready for school. Then she sat down on the floor next to Jude, among the pieces of cereal.

'Jude's OK, Addie,' she said, even though he wasn't.

Ruth rested one hand on Jude's ankle. Addie saw him take a big breath in and hold it. His shoulders shook. Addie knew that he was trying to push something back down deep inside. Into the hollow place where the tears stay.

She got down from the table. She couldn't look at him any more.

SIX

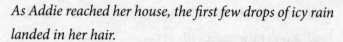

As Addie reached her house, the first few drops of icy rain landed in her hair.

There was no sound from behind the front door. Addie rummaged in her coat pocket for her key. It had slipped through the hole and into the lining. Again. She needed to remember about that hole. Her tummy rumbled as she pinned her bread and milk under one arm, and wriggled the key free from the coat lining. Her cold fingers were clumsy, slow. The carton of milk slid from her grasp, bounced on the broken edge of the step and exploded like a white bomb on the gravel path. Milk splashed the air, trickled between the tiny stones. Addie watched it disappear.

So much for breakfast.

No more milk. No more money.

She'd really done it now.

She scooped up the empty carton and hurried inside before anyone could see. She sat down at the bottom of *the stairs, stared up at the clay figures on the bookshelf beside her. She remembered the softness of the clay in her hands, the warmth of Mam's fingers on her own as they pushed and pulled the figures in to life. The clay people stared past her with their empty eyes.*

Hail rattled on the window, doors slammed, children called, cars stuttered into life.

The letterbox lifted; fell.

Mam slept on.

Then the siren, coloured lights splitting the frost on the window: spinning across the floor; spinning over Addie.

Heavy boots on the gravel, the ring, ring, ring of the doorbell, the thump of fists on the door.

Who had told? Darren's mam? Mrs Crabtree?

It didn't matter. It was too late now anyway.

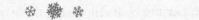

Addie opened the blue-handled drawers and gathered up her neatly folded clothes. She stuffed them into her bag.

'You'll only have to put it all back,' Sunni said. She pulled a navy sweatshirt over her head. 'You'll see.'

Addie ignored her. She didn't know anything.

31

'And don't ever put stuff on my shelf again. All right?'

Something flew past Addie's ear as she bent over her bag. Jude's green cup. It hit the wall, fell on to Addie's bed. She reached for it, felt the weight of it in her hand. She could throw it right back at Sunni. She wouldn't miss.

'All right?' Sunni poked her finger hard into Addie's back.

Addie glared at her over one shoulder, squeezed the cup hard. 'I'm *going home*. I *told* you.' She clenched her teeth so tightly that a pain shot up her cheek.

'Whatever. Hang your bag up behind the door. I like my room tidy.' Sunni stalked out of the room and slammed the door behind her.

Addie stared at Sunni's stupid shelf, with its stupid family of stupid elephants. She pushed the biggest one with her finger. It fell, taking three others with it. They slid into a heap of legs, trunks, and shiny, black bead eyes. A small china horse slid with them and fell to the floor. Addie pushed at the broken pieces with the toe of her trainer, hid them under Sunni's bed. Served her right.

She went to the bathroom. She rinsed and dried Jude's cup and put it back exactly where she'd found it. She splashed water on her face, caught sight of herself in the mirror above the sink – saw the usual smudges under her eyes, the usual wild frizz of hair. She dried herself on someone's pink towel and tugged her fingers through her tightly knotted curls. Her dad's curls. She hated the reminder of him. Hated him. Why couldn't she have had Mam's hair?

She went downstairs, treading softly. She hoped Sunni had left for school. She never wanted to see her again. Ever.

Her coat was hanging on a peg in the hall. It was dry now. She pushed her arms into it and turned up the collar. She would wait outside for her lift home with Penny.

The front door was unlocked, but old and stiff. Addie tugged it open as quietly as she could. Icy air swept across her ankles. She shivered in her thin coat, pulled the zip right up to the top and felt in the pocket for her gloves. They weren't there. She peered out into the yard to see if anyone was about.

Sunni rushed up behind her. She was muffled in a purple padded coat, her dark hair hidden under a furry hood. Her boots clattered across the floor: short, shiny black boots with buckles. Just like the ones Mam had promised Addie for her last birthday.

Addie was glad she didn't get them now.

'Mind out,' Sunni said. She pushed past Addie in the doorway, making the door bang against the wall. 'Mira's dad's picking me up,' she said, looking back over her shoulder. 'We're having a sleepover after school.'

'Like I care,' Addie said, as she watched Sunni run across the courtyard. She slipped twice, almost fell over. Addie wished she *had* fallen. How come she even *had* any friends?

Before Addie could step outside, the kitchen door swung open. Ruth.

'Addie, sweetheart, it's not really the weather for being outside.'

'I'm looking out for Penny's car. I'm fine.'

Ruth shut the door. 'Penny just rang, Addie.'

'What time's she getting here?'

Ruth smiled. That smile adults used when they were about to say something Addie wouldn't like. The icy air was inside Addie's clothes now, curling round her heart.

'Come on into the kitchen, love,' Ruth said. 'We need a bit of a chat.' She ushered Addie through the kitchen door, like she was one of her chickens.

Jude was still there. He was sitting up at the table with crayons and paper, but he wasn't drawing anything. Addie thought of Mam, in front of her easel, creating sequins of light on a bright blue sea. She thought of the light in Mam's eyes: how it wasn't there any more.

Ruth sat down on a rocking chair by the fireplace. She patted her hand on a green chair next to her.

Addie didn't sit down. 'What did Penny say?' she said. 'Is she on her way?'

She already knew the answer.

'Penny can't make it today, Addie. She's got an emergency to deal with. And the roads are dreadful.' She reached over, put her hand on Addie's arm.

Addie shrugged it away.

'She's very sorry, Addie, but she'll be here as soon as she can with the rest of your things.'

'I don't need any things! I'm going home. Today.'

'Penny will explain everything, Addie, and answer all your questions. Tomorrow, hopefully,' Ruth said. She glanced towards the window. 'If the snow doesn't get any worse. It's stopped for now, but Sam says it's pretty thick out on the moorland roads. He and Gabe are out there on a rescue mission this morning . . .'

Ruth's words came from far away, muffled, like she was speaking underwater.

Who was going to rescue *Addie*?

'Mam won't be OK without me,' she said.

'Your mam needs some special help just now, Addie.' Ruth smiled that smile again. 'I think you know that, don't you? Better than anyone.'

Addie shook her head. 'You can't keep me here,' she shouted. She kicked the green chair, making it skid towards the fire. A log shifted in the fireplace, sending sparks into the air, like tiny yellow flares. Ruth's phone rang again.

Jude gave another of his thin, wild wails. He threw his box of crayons. Splinters of colour flew through the air, spread across the floor. He stared up at Addie as she strode past the table, his eyes empty, like the sheet of paper in front of him. Empty like Addie.

Addie was going home today, whatever Ruth and Penny said. She edged round the front door, stepped outside and looked around.

Old stone buildings surrounded the courtyard,

skeletal trees beyond. Someone had cleared a pathway through the snow near the door. Under Addie's feet were grey cobbles, dusted white – the sparkle of ice where light from the farmhouse touched them. Above her, a wide grey sky: smoky, like dirty paintbrush water. It seemed to go on forever.

A single, soft flake drifted past Addie's cheek, a tiny white star against the gloom. She reached out; felt it light as air in the palm of her hand. Then it was gone.

Was more snow coming? Addie hoped not. She blew on her hands, wrapped her arms round herself and took a deep breath in. Which way was home?

She trudged in the direction Sunni had gone to be picked up, snow spilling over the tops of her trainers. She peered round the side of the old stone barn. A huge gate swung open. Beyond it, a rough road, lined with spiky hedges and the leafless trees, dark and harsh against the white landscape.

Addie glanced behind her. No one was coming. Yet. She set off down the track.

SEVEN

Addie had only been walking a few minutes when it started to snow again. No gentle flakes this time, just sudden gusts of ice and sleet. They whirled through the bony trees, stole the last colour from the world around Addie. Bitter air stung her chest as she breathed in; nipped at her fingers like terrible teeth. Her feet burned with cold.

Mam hadn't told the truth in her soft sketches. Snow was sharp. Snow was cruel.

She thought about last night's long drive with Penny, remembered the misty moorland and shadowy forests. Ruth and Sam's farm was in the middle of nowhere. What was she doing out here?

She stood still, looked back, half hoping to see Ruth coming down the track to find her. But there was no one. Just her own footprints, quickly filling with snow. No sound except the drum of her heart in her ears and the moan of an animal, carried on the wind. A cow,

Addie told herself. But dark, nameless shapes slipped across her mind.

A huge black bird lifted from the ground ahead. It perched on a branch above Addie, yellow eyes glaring down through the thick, white air; daring her to steal a half-finished meal abandoned on the snow. Addie stepped round the pink muddle of blood and fur, glared back at the hunched bird.

'Horrible creature! Devil bird!' she shouted.

She hated this winter world and everything in it.

But she couldn't go back to the warm farmhouse. Mam needed her. There had to be a bus stop *somewhere* near the farm, didn't there?

Addie bent her head against the weather, pinned her hands under her armpits for warmth and set off again.

The track forked in front of her. Nothing but moorland and trees in both directions. Which way should she go?

She went right. A few minutes later, the track divided into two again, one narrow limb disappearing among a glade of snow-laden pines. Now what?

Then she saw them, weaving between the trees. A tall boy, hands in the pockets of a heavy jacket, dark beanie hat crusted with snow. A black and white dog, its nose to the ground as it moved in quick circles through the snow-covered undergrowth.

The dog looked up, spotted Addie. It darted towards her, jumped up, and almost knocked her flying.

'Flo! Here!' The boy whistled, patted his leg.

The dog raced to his side, trotted next to him as he plodded along the track towards Addie. This must be Ruth's son then. What was his name? Addie couldn't remember. Was he out here looking for *her*?

And if he was, what would he do now that he'd found her?

He stopped; grinned.

It *was* him. She'd seen that face – a younger version, smiling through gappy teeth on the fridge door in Ruth's kitchen.

'Adelaide, by any chance?' he said. He held out a gloved hand, made a silly bow. 'Gabe,' he said. 'Ruth and Sam's son.'

Addie ignored him, looked down at Flo. The dog stared up at her with amber eyes and wagged her tail, sending a shower of snow crystals into the air

'And this is Flo,' Gabe said.

Addie reached down and stroked the dog's silky head. She looked up at Gabe.

'C'mon then,' Gabe said, indicating with his head that Addie should move. 'Ma's about to get the Search and Rescue guys out.'

Addie shrugged; folded her arms across her chest. 'I'm getting a bus,' she said.

'OK. Right.' Gabe nodded. 'Two miles that way then.' He pointed through the pine trees. 'Should be one along in about . . . let me think –' he scratched his chin – 'twenty-four hours.' He gazed up at the laden sky. 'Weather permitting.'

'Very funny.' Addie pressed her lips together to still the quiver she felt there. She turned away.

'Suit yourself.' Gabe took off a glove, brought a phone out of his pocket, held it out and moved it around him. 'No signal. Damn. Oh, well . . .'

He whistled for Flo again and set off in the direction Addie had walked. 'Shame, though,' he called over his shoulder. 'I was counting on your help . . .'

Addie wasn't falling for that one. Did he think she was stupid?

'Tiny wild foal,' he shouted. 'Found him first thing, stuck in the snow. Frozen, he was. Scared half to death.' He lifted his arms, let them drop. 'Back at the farm now, but dunno if he'll make it.' He turned, walked backwards, yelling against the wind.

'Lucky Flo found him at all. He was even more lost than you are . . .'

EIGHT

Addie stared at Gabe's back as he trudged away, bent against the snow that was now slicing sideways though the air. He was actually leaving her there. Well, that was fine. He had probably lied about the bus just to scare her into going back with him. People still needed buses, even in the middle of nowhere. Especially in the middle of nowhere. And buses were big enough to get through a bit of snow. Anyway, she *wasn't* lost. Not really. She could go back the way she'd come any time she wanted.

She set off towards the glade of pines. A thick cluster of snow slid from the branches of the first tree as she approached; thumped to the ground just in front of her. She stopped.

What if Gabe was telling the truth? She wouldn't survive a night out here. And then what would happen to Mam? She'd better go back. Just for now. She would make a better plan.

'Hold on a minute! Gabe!' she called. But her words

were whisked away on the wind. Even Flo wouldn't hear her in this weather. She shielded her eyes with her hand; spat snow from her lips. She could barely see a few feet ahead. Gabe wouldn't have got far. She set off, following his tracks as best she could.

He was leaning against a great fir tree round the first bend, ankles crossed, head bent over his phone. Flo stood at his feet, ears pricked high. She ran towards Addie, swerved behind her and nosed at her leg until she was face to face with Gabe.

'Couldn't get her to move,' Gabe said, without looking up. 'Must've known you were coming.' He stuffed his phone in his pocket, scratched Flo's head. 'Happy now, girl?'

Flo stared up at Gabe, looked back at Addie, her red tongue lolling from the side of her mouth. Addie could have sworn she was smiling.

Ruth hurried Addie into the hall. She fussed and flapped, held Addie at arm's-length, inspected her for damage.

Gabe stamped snow from his boots and stepped inside. 'She's good, Ma. No probs.' He pulled off his hat, shook it into the yard behind him. He looked younger without it, Addie thought, his flame-red hair a mess of wild waves. He raised an eyebrow at her. 'Just having a look round, weren't you, Adelaide?' he said. 'Lost your bearings a bit.'

Addie glared at him. 'It's Addie. I *told* you,' she said, and turned away. She didn't need him to make excuses for her. She could stick up for herself.

'I was checking for bus stops,' she told Ruth, her chin in the air. 'In case Penny can't get here in her car.'

Addie saw Ruth's eyes slide towards Gabe, saw them meet with his. 'And I'm fine,' she said. She stared down at her sodden trainers, at the pools of water collecting around them on the tiled floor. She tried to take off her coat, but her arms felt stiff, useless. Her teeth started to chatter. She couldn't make them stop

Ruth kneeled down in front of her. 'Let's just get you warm, shall we? A nice bath, that's what's needed.' She eased Addie's coat from her shoulders. 'Then some soup.' She reached for Gabe's hand. 'Both of you, I think.'

'Resistance is futile,' said Gabe. He grinned at Addie. 'Trust me. I know.' He whistled for Flo.

'No you don't, Flo,' said Ruth. She laughed. 'She'd be in the shower with him, if I let her, Addie.' She threw a towel over Flo, began to rub her dry.

'Saves water, Ma,' said Gabe. 'Like you did in the war.'

Ruth flicked the towel at him. He skipped out of her reach and into the hall.

'Nice thick towels on your bed, Addie,' Ruth called, as Addie left the room. And you're OK to use the main bathroom. Gabe has his own shower.'

Gabe took the stairs two at a time and disappeared before Addie had hauled herself up the first two steps. As she waited for her bath to fill, she heard him clatter back down again. He was singing. A silly, jumbled song, loud and out of tune.

Addie saw herself – a tiny girl, whirling across the living-room floor in front of Mam. She caught the click-clack of her new red tap shoes, the silver glint of Christmas tinsel in Mam's hair; heard her own small voice lifting on the air in tuneless song – just like Gabe's. She remembered the joy of it; remembered Mam's smile – bright, beautiful: the centre of the world. She slipped down lower into the bath, let the water slide across her face and tried to hold that smile behind her tightly closed eyes.

NINE

Gabe stood in the kitchen doorway, grubby Wellington boots in one hand.

'You coming to help this morning, or what?'

Addie shook her head. She shuffled further into the window seat, tucked her knees up under her chin.

'It's still snowing,' she said.

'Yep,' Gabe said. 'So we're busier than ever.'

'When's it going to stop?'

Gabe dropped the boots, stuffed his hands in his coat pockets and pulled out the linings. 'Sorry,' he said. 'Lost it again.'

Addie stared at him.

'My crystal ball.'

Addie shut her eyes. Why didn't he leave her alone?

'OK. You just sit there in your PJs. You'll feel so much better.'

'What would you know?'

'Not much. Obviously.' Gabe scratched his head,

made his hair stand on end. 'Really need you today, that's all. Dad's been on the phone to Jo. She can't get through either, with the snow. But she says that foal's got to take some feed today, or . . .'

Addie looked up. 'Jo?'

'Vet. Someone's got to sit with him, Addie. Get him used to human company.'

'So?'

'You're the chosen one. Everyone else is busy.'

Addie turned away, stared at the frost ferns on the window. She should be sitting with Mam. Helping Mam.

'No good him getting used to me,' she said. 'I'm going once the snow clears a bit.'

'Yeah. You said.' Gabe sighed. 'I'll have to wait for Sunni then, I suppose.'

'Sunni's back? Already?'

Gabe took his beanie hat from the back pocket of his jeans, pulled it on. 'Will be. Dad's gone for her in the jeep.'

Great, Addie thought. As if her day wasn't bad enough already. She stood up. 'All right. I'll come,' she said. 'Just this once. It won't like me, though, that foal.'

It was dark inside the barn after the brilliance of the white world outside.

'Stand still for a bit,' Gabe said, his voice low. 'Let your eyes adjust. And move slowly.'

Addie squinted, looked around. Daylight crept through cracked walls, criss-crossed the barn. Dust whirled in the needles of light. There was a sweet, musty smell. Addie could make out mounds of straw draped in heavy cloth and some wooden stalls at the back of the building.

Gabe tugged at her sleeve, held his finger to his lips and walked slowly towards a stall on the left-hand side. A lamp, fixed at one side, shed soft yellow light on the walls, lit great cobwebs that hung like dirty rags from the rafters above.

The foal was curled under a pile of blankets in a corner of the pen, his dark, shaggy head just visible. He shifted as Addie and Gabe came close and pushed his pale muzzle into the corner. The blankets rose and fell with his panicked breaths.

'He's really scared,' Addie whispered. 'He doesn't like us being here.'

'No. But he needs us,' Gabe said. 'If he's gonna make it.' He glanced around, disappeared for a moment inside

49

the next stall; reappeared with his arms full of straw. 'Help me get some more,' he said. 'Extra warmth.'

The straw was scratchy against Addie's skin. Her nose itched as she carried armfuls, spread it around the foal like Gabe showed her. She pinched her nostrils to stifle a sneeze.

Gabe gathered some of the clean straw into a small heap close to where the foal lay. He spread an empty sack on top of it. 'There you go,' he said, gesturing for her to sit down. 'Fit for a queen. I've got to go and mix up his feed. Won't be long.'

'What am I supposed to do?'

'Talk to him.'

'And say what?'

Gabe shook his head, blew through his teeth. 'Anything. Reassure him. You'll figure it out.' He brushed dust and straw from his jacket. 'Oh, and I'll have to find Dad, get the antibiotics the vet left us when she knew the snow was forecast.' He crept away, stopped halfway across the barn; came back. 'Don't tell Ma I left you on your own, or I'm done for.' He held two fingers to his head, pretended to shoot.

He *was* bonkers. Sunni was right about that, at least.

The foal stiffened as Addie sat down. His breath came in short rasps.

'You're all right,' Addie said. 'I'll move away a bit.' She shuffled backwards and rested her back against the wall of the pen. The foal quivered and squirmed. Addie was making him worse. She didn't know anything about animals, especially wild ones.

'Gabe will be back in a minute,' she said. 'With your food.'

The foal pressed himself further into the corner.

'Not hungry, are you? Me neither.' She picked up two blades of straw, twisted them together. 'You've got to eat, though. Just a bit, OK?'

Addie chewed at the ends of the straw. They tasted bitter. She spat saliva on to the floor. The foal jumped, quivered even more.

How long was Gabe going to be? She couldn't stay long, anyway. Penny said she might ring again after she'd had her meeting. Was she there now? What was she saying about Mam? Addie rested her chin on her knees, felt it tremble. She wiped her eyes with her sleeve; sniffed. The foal lifted its head a little, rested it back down again.

'Want your mam too, don't you?' Addie said, her

words ragged, thin. She covered her face with her hands and tried to control her own breathing. When she moved them away, the foal was staring at her, his wide dark eyes shimmering in the yellow light.

'Hello,' Addie said.

The foal stretched his neck towards her, struggled to move his body free of the blankets. Addie saw that his mane was wild with knots and caked with mud. A shrivelled leaf clung there.

She slid down on to the straw and reached towards him, her hand hovering, unsure. The foal nudged it with a velvet nose, then rested his head on her knee. It was as light as air; barely there at all. Addie kept still; hardly dared to breathe. She watched his long eyelashes flutter and close; smelled his earthy scent.

'That's it,' she whispered. 'You just sleep.'

TEN

'It's amazing,' Sam told Ruth. 'Not even Gabe could get near that foal.'

Ruth looked up from her mixing bowl, pointed towards Addie with a buttery spoon. 'Well done, Addie,' she said. 'You've got the magic touch.'

Sunni bounced into the kitchen. A rainbow-bright bag swung from her shoulder.

'Who has?' she said.

Addie shrugged. 'I just sat there,' she told Sam.

'Oh, *her*,' Sunni said. She flung herself on to the chair opposite Addie; glared at her.

Gabe took off his jacket. He leaned over Ruth's shoulder, stuck a finger into her mixing bowl and wandered across to Sunni. He placed a dollop of yellow cake mixture on her nose and grinned at Addie. 'Like I said, Addie, you're the chosen one.'

'I wouldn't choose *her* for anything,' Sunni muttered. She shook the contents of her bag on to the table.

A purple slipper and a torn magazine fell to the floor.

'Dirty clothes in the washer, please, Sunni,' Ruth said. 'And let's try to be kind, shall we?'

Sam raised his eyebrows at Sunni. She bundled her nightdress, jumper and jeans back into the bag, picked up her magazine. 'So-*rry*,' she said.

She wasn't.

No one was ever sorry. Not the boys in Addie's street, with their sharp, twisting finger burns on her skin. Not the girls who blew smoke in her face outside Mr Borovski's shop, and called her mam names as she hurried past them.

Addie lifted her chin and looked away. Sunni wasn't important. But just let her say *one thing* about her mam.

Sam sat down, held his hands towards the fire. 'What Gabe means, Addie, is that it's something special – that sort of affinity with a wild creature. That foal's so young and scared, too. To be honest, we thought he would shut down and give up. So did the vet.'

'Better hang around a bit after all, Addie,' Sunni said. 'Or he might die.' She picked up her magazine, flicked through the pages. 'No pressure.'

Sam glanced at Ruth. He looked back at Sunni, his

mouth a firm line. 'How much sleep did you get at Mira's, young lady?'

Sunni shrugged.

'Gabe, how about you give Sunni another guitar lesson?' Ruth said. 'She needs something to do, I think.'

'Come on then, trouble,' Gabe said. 'Long as you promise not to play better than me this time.'

'Lunch in half an hour, mind,' Ruth called as Sunni jumped to her feet. She put a tray of muffin cases on the table. 'Perhaps you'd like to help me with these, Addie. Then we can ice them later.'

'I'm tired,' said Addie. 'No. Thanks.'

'It's all that pony whispering,' said Sam. 'Hard work.' He stretched back in the chair, crossed his ankles and ran his hands over his shock of dark hair. Addie watched him. He seemed so calm and relaxed. Was he always that way?

Addie jumped as Ruth slammed the oven door closed.

'Don't let me forget those cakes, Addie,' she said. 'They're a new recipe. I'm practising for Jude's birthday cake.'

'It's his birthday?' said Addie. 'When? Is his mam coming?'

'No, love, she isn't.' But we'll make it really special for

him, won't we?' She smiled at Addie. 'Its next month. Soon be here.'

Addie put her head in her hands. Why wasn't anybody listening? She wasn't going to be here next month. She wasn't going to be here for even one more day.

Sam shifted in his chair, cleared his throat. Ruth's hand was on Addie's shoulder.

Addie pulled away and clattered up the stairs. She threw herself on her bed, listened to the twang of Sunni's guitar through the wall. Gabe's voice rose and fell; Sunni giggled. Addie curled in a tight ball and thought of the foal under his blankets in the dark barn. She hoped he wouldn't give up and fade away now that she'd left him all alone.

ELEVEN

The snow didn't stop the next day or the one after that. Penny didn't come.

She rang, said that she'd be there just as soon as the snow let up a bit. She said Mam sent her love and that she was doing OK. Her voice went up at the end of the sentence, like she was making that bit it up – wishing that it was true.

The rain arrived on Saturday. And Penny was coming, too. Even though it was the weekend. Addie didn't know if that was a good sign or a bad one. Jude's social worker, Tim, was giving Penny a lift in his special jeep, which was good for winter weather. Addie wondered why nobody had thought of that before.

Her stomach tightened every time she thought about what Penny might say when she got here.

Might she take Addie home, after all?

Addie couldn't swallow her toast at breakfast. She didn't feel like talking, so she curled up on the window seat and pretended to read. Rain hit the window in fat circles, then ran to the sill in crazy rivers; stole the frost feathers from the glass. Addie kept an eye on the tall clock by the door. Its black hands never seemed to move.

Ruth brought Jude into the kitchen, fresh from the shower. His hair twisted in damp ringlets on his forehead. His wide blue eyes scanned the room and held Addie's for a small moment.

'Jude's going to help make some scones, aren't you?' Ruth said. 'Penny and Tim can have some with their coffee.' She put an enormous mixing bowl on the table. 'Want to help, Addie?' She went to a cupboard, began piling ingredients on the bench and took milk from the fridge.

'Dunno,' Addie said. Social workers drank lots of coffee. She knew that. But she wasn't sure they should get scones to go with it.

Jude sat down at the table, his face barely visible above the rim of the bowl. He stared at Addie, wooden spoon in hand.

'OK then,' Addie said. 'I suppose.'

She and Jude stirred butter and sugar, piled glistening cherries into the bowl. It was hard work. Addie's arms ached.

Jude held the sieve while she tipped in flour bit by bit. It lifted in a white cloud when he shook the sieve, dusted their wrists and hands. Addie faked a huge sneeze. Jude's lips twitched, as if he might smile. He didn't. Maybe he had forgotten how to do that too.

'Goodness,' Ruth said, laughing, 'it's snowing indoors now!'

She showed them how to push the sticky mixture from the spoon with one finger; how to make little piles on silver trays for the oven. Jude screamed at Ruth about a speck of mixture on his T-shirt. Ruth took him upstairs to change.

Addie thought they would be a while. That was the only T-shirt Jude had agreed to wear since Addie arrived. She went back to the window seat and peered through the blur of rain into the yard. She breathed in the warm smell of the scones as they baked. She tried to remember the last time she had baked with Mam – kneeling on a chair to reach the table, feeling the crack of eggshell under her thumb, the yellow stickiness of yolk between her fingers and running down her arm.

She heard Mam's voice. 'Go on, never mind, Addie. Try another . . .'

She thought of the eggs in Ruth and Sam's henhouse; of the mother hens, with their nodding heads and ugly claws, their wing feathers softly spread to protect their babies inside those fragile shells.

She tried to hear Mam's voice again. It wouldn't come.

Feet thundered down the stairs and the kitchen door swung wide. It banged against the wall. Sunni struggled in, laptop clutched to her chest, books and a bunch of papers tucked under her arm. She slid the laptop on to the table and thumped the books down. Pieces of paper slid to the floor.

'Don't help then,' she said.

'OK,' Addie said. 'I won't.' She shrugged. 'Anyway, Ruth said you had to work in the bedroom. On your own.' She hoped that Ruth wouldn't be gone too long after all.

Ruth appeared a minute or two later, holding a red-faced Jude by the hand. He was still wearing his Batman T-shirt. It had a dark, wet patch right across Batman's face. Jude was holding the damp material away from his body, his nose wrinkled in disgust.

'Sit here, Jude,' Ruth said, pointing to the rocking chair

by the fire. 'It'll dry before Tim gets here, don't worry.'

'He won't be here for ages,' said Sunni. 'The roads will be even worse now, all icy under the snow. His jeep will probably get stuck.'

Addie glared at her. Sunni flicked her hair over her shoulders and bent over her books. 'Mira's dad said,' she added, as if that meant it must be true. 'He does loads of driving.'

'I think they'll be fine, Sunni,' Ruth said. She smiled at Addie and Jude. 'Tim's car has special tyres for the snow, hasn't it, Jude? It'll get icy overnight, for sure. But not yet.' She handed Sunni a glass of milk. 'You might be better off in your room, Sunni, love,' she said, 'or in the snug. You need to concentrate on that homework and get it finished.'

'Don't see why I have to do it anyway,' Sunni said. 'On a Saturday.'

'Because you didn't want to do it on a Friday!' Ruth laughed, shook her head. 'I don't know! See how you get on at the table in here then. But no annoying the other two, or back you go.'

Sunni smirked at Addie, sat down and opened the laptop. Addie turned away; listened to the tap of Sunni's fingers on the keys, the clatter of tins, the surge of the water, as Ruth washed the baking things in the sink. Ruth was always so busy. Addie should offer to help. She didn't.

Jude curled up in the rocking chair, his knees under his chin. Widget jumped on his lap. He pushed him off, brushed at his trousers. Addie watched him rock back and forth; back and forth. The wooden rockers ticked off the seconds on the tiled floor.

Sunni looked up from the laptop and slammed it shut. 'I'm too tired,' she said. She pointed at Addie with her pen. 'Why doesn't she have to do school work?' She pulled her mouth down at the edges. 'Think you're so lucky, Addie,' she said. 'But you're going to get miles behind everyone else. Not so lucky then.'

Ruth shook her head. 'What did I say, Sunni?' She smiled an apology at Addie. Her eyes were kind; crinkled at the corners. 'You'll be fine, Addie,' she said. 'We'll make sure you catch up before you go. You can join Gabe for his home-school sessions, if you like. It'll be fun, I promise.'

'Right,' Sunni said. She snorted, looked away.

Ruth dried her hands on a red-spotted tea towel. 'You're really a kind girl, Sunni, I know. So let's have no more of that. Come on, show me how far you've got.'

She sat down next to Sunni, opened the laptop and rested an arm across Sunni's shoulders.

'I like school work,' Addie said. 'I like school. If I wasn't stuck out here, I'd be there.' She stretched out on the window seat, folded her arms behind her head. 'And I wouldn't keep moaning about homework.'

She missed school. She did.

School the way it used to be.

She remembered her first classrooms: the rainbow colours, the clamour of voices, the books with their secrets and puzzles. The new words that stretched her tongue; the new ideas that made her brain fizz. She remembered the shiny corridors, the smell of polish and roast potatoes; the soft, sticky warmth of Hattie's hand in hers as they skipped on summer grass.

Hattie. Her best friend. Forever.

She saw herself standing on the playground wall next to Hattie, arms outstretched: a small tightrope walker, balanced and sure, the sun warm on her bare arms. She tried to hold the memory, to be that Addie again, there in Ruth's kitchen.

The memory blurred; trickled away like the rivers of rain on the window. The tightrope walker was gone.

She saw herself sitting on the playground wall,

swinging her legs as if everything was fine. She saw Hattie, watched her run hand in hand with Lola Smythe.

She saw Daren Oates and his stupid mates, heard their jeering calls:

'Hey, Adelaide Forgettable Jones!'

'Where's your mam this time, then?'

'Oh, wait. Everyone knows where *she'll* be . . .'

The front door clicked open, wrenched Addie from the memory. Boots stamped in the hallway.

Addie felt sick. Really sick. She chewed at her nails.

The door slammed shut again.

'No sign yet,' Sam shouted. 'I'll just get out of these clothes.'

Jude sighed. Addie glanced over at him. His head was tucked down low on his chest, his eyes fixed straight ahead. He was waiting too, hunched and huddled like the cold birds on the barn roof. Addie wished she could cheer him up. She didn't know how.

Ruth was next to her, a large cardboard box under one arm.

'You OK, there?' she said. 'Miles away, eh?'

Addie nodded.

'Have a look through these,' Ruth said. She opened the flaps of the box. 'Come on, Jude. You too. Best keep busy while you both wait. And your turn for the laptop too, Addie, if you like. Sunni needs to work from her books for a bit.'

'Typical,' Sunni said. She picked up a book, pushed it away again.

Addie got up. 'Thanks,' she said. Anything to make the time go quicker. Anything to annoy Sunni. She crossed to the table.

The box was crammed with craft materials: cracked lumps of clay wrapped in film, pots of modelling dough – green, pink and blue, a ball of striped string, bundles of ribbon, buttons in a jar and rolls of rough grey paper. 'Look, Jude,' she said. 'Clay and stuff. Come and see.'

Jude didn't move. Perhaps he would come if she ignored him.

Addie spread the contents of the box on the table for him to see. She opened the laptop. She typed 'Exmoor' into the search bar. Maybe she could find out exactly where she was. How far she was from home.

She scrolled through pages of text, complicated maps and shots of moorland: summer green, with a wide blue sky that Addie could not imagine here; red and gold autumn scenes, a haze of purple heather across sloping fields. And, of course, the ice-white winter stillness that she already knew so well.

There were grainy black and white photographs of tall stones like the ones Addie had seen in a book about Stonehenge. Crumbling buildings, shepherds with long beards and thin pipes, dogs like Flo. And ponies. Herds of brown ponies with dark tangled manes and black almond-shaped eyes. A tiny foal feeding from its red-coated mother. A group of larger foals leaping on strong black legs. Their coats were sleek and smooth: nothing like the shaggy chaos that covered the foal in the barn. *Exmoor youngsters in their summer coats,* Addie read, *having fun together under the watchful eyes of their mothers and their herd.*

Jude was beside her. She smiled at him.

'Exmoor ponies, Jude. Look. Like the one Flo and Gabe found in the snow.'

Jude stared at the screen. He pointed at the small foal with its mother. His thin finger trembled. The images on the screen swam. Addie closed the page and pushed the laptop away.

'How about we make one – a pony – out of clay?' she said. 'And a boy, like you, for its friend?'

Jude sat down. Next to Addie. He reached for a ball of clay and rolled it towards her.

TWELVE

Eleven o'clock. Still no Penny and Tim.

Gabe appeared at the window, his face distorted by the rain. He knocked, pressed his nose against the glass.

Ruth opened the window. A blast of cold, damp air rushed into the kitchen.

'Sorry, Ma,' Gabe said. 'Can't come in. Pig-pen boots. Particularly rich in there today.' He wiped raindrops from strands of hair that had escaped from his sodden beanie hat, and looked across at Sunni.

'The foal needs you, Addie. He still won't take his breakfast from me. I tried twice, but I don't match up. Obviously.'

'I'll come,' Addie said. She was glad to escape the kitchen with its slowly ticking clock; glad to escape the warm, sweet smells that made her feel nauseous today. 'Bet I'll be finished before Penny even gets here.'

'Get some proper waterproofs on,' Gabe said. 'Or you'll be looking as good as me – difficult though that would be.' He turned up his collar. 'I'll go and do the hens, Ma, while Addie works her magic on the foal. Save you getting soaked later, as well.' He pushed the window shut.

Addie left Jude with his clay figures. She would make more later, she promised. Unless Penny was taking her home.

Addie squeezed round the barn door. 'Only me,' she said.

The foal whinnied softly. His pale muzzle appeared at the edge of his stall. He struggled to his feet as Addie came close, pushed up with his long back legs and unfolded his front ones – slowly – as if it was still a puzzle to get them all to work together.

'Well done,' Addie said.

He took a tentative step towards her, nudged the bucket in her hands.

'You want this first? Go on then.'

Addie put the bucket of mixed feed on the straw in front of him. She rested the bottle of milk on the makeshift seat Gabe had made her. The foal's head disappeared inside the bucket. She watched him eat. His jaws slid from side to side as he chewed; his teeth scraped at the metal base of the bucket.

'You're starving today, aren't you?' she said.

The foal looked up at Addie. Bits of mixed meal clung to his lashes and decorated his nose. He blinked, shook his head; wobbled on his thin legs.

Addie reached for the bottle of milk Gabe had given her. 'Want your drink now?' she said.

He drank in long gulps, pulling hard on the rubber teat. He was getting stronger. Addie had to hold the bottle with both hands.

'Thirsty as well as hungry? Good boy,' she said. She leaned forward and brushed some grain from the foal's left eye with her finger. He jumped away, startled.

'Sorry, sorry,' Addie said. 'It's OK.'

The foal shifted from side to side. His thin legs trembled. His eyes were wide, glinting white at the corners. She had gone too far.

'It's OK,' Addie said. 'Finish your breakfast. You've got to get strong.'

She offered the bottle again, spoke gently to the foal. He stared up at her, searched her face for a moment; began to drink again. When he had finished, he sank down on to the straw, his head resting across Addie's left boot. She stood still, afraid to upset him again. His head became heavier. His breathing slowed. He slept.

Addie watched his body rise and fall. Every so often he flinched, his legs shifting underneath him. Perhaps he was dreaming: dreaming of his mam, running in his sleep towards her.

Addie's foot became numb. Pins and needles crept up her ankle. She would have to move. She slid one foot from under the foal's chin. He opened one eye, closed it and resettled himself on the straw. Addie slipped down next to him, her back against the wall. She wriggled her toes back to life.

How long had she been here? It didn't matter. Someone would have come for her if Penny had arrived.

Maybe she didn't even want to see Penny. She clutched at the straw under her hands, gathered a clump of it and tightened her fist round it. Her nails dug into her palm. When she opened her fist, bent strands of straw slowly unfolded like broken insect legs. She brushed them away.

She hated Penny. Penny and her promises. Penny and her lies about Mam.

The foal was sound asleep. His soft breaths blew dust from the straw around his nostrils. Addie laid a hand on his neck. His coat was thick and wiry. She wriggled her fingers through his mane and the rope of coarse hair across his back. She felt the knots and dried mud that clung there.

'You've got worse tangles than me,' she whispered.

What colour would he be, she wondered, under all the dirt? Would he look more like the foals in those photographs when summer came? Addie wouldn't be here to know. She would ask Ruth to send her a picture. 'Better get you cleaned up soon,' she said. 'Before I go home.'

The foal opened one eye, then the other. He fixed Addie with his deep gaze. Addie saw her own face, blurred and tiny in each of his black eyes.

He blew softly down his nose, lifted his head and laid it across her knees. His breaths lengthened again. His warmth seeped into Addie's limbs. She closed her eyes.

Addie jumped awake. The foal scrabbled to his feet. His eyes were wide. His ears stiffened; twitched.

The barn door scraped open. Light flooded in. Icy wind and rain whipped across the floor. Straw lifted, dust spiralled. The foal scrambled to the back of the stall, legs sliding in opposite directions.

'You're all right,' Addie said gently. 'I'm here.' She stepped in front of him, pressed herself against his flank, shielding him. The thump of his heart vibrated through her body.

'Sorry, mate,' Gabe said. He sighed. 'Poor little guy.' He nodded at the empty bucket; the bottle on its side in the straw. He smiled at Addie. 'Took all his feed, though?'

'Yep,' Addie said. 'And he was having a good sleep. Till you got here.'

'Message from Ma,' Gabe said, ignoring the jibe. He pulled off his beanie hat. Orange today. It clashed horribly with his red hair. 'Penny'll be here in forty-five minutes, tops.'

Addie shrugged. 'You scared the foal,' she said.

Gabe nodded. 'Maybe it's the hat he doesn't like,' he said. 'Flo was really freaked by hats when she was a pup. And umbrellas. And pigs.'

'Reasonable,' Addie said. 'About the pigs.'

Sam had shown her the pigs on the farm. Massive, filthy, snuffling, beady-eyed things. 'And the hats,' she said. 'Actually, especially the hats.' She pointed at the orange beanie, felt a smile pull at her lips.

Gabe held it out in front of him. He laughed. 'This is my favourite, though! My nan made it for me.'

'Your nan?' Addie said. 'Does she live round here, too?'

Gabe looked away. 'She died.' He folded the hat and pushed it into his pocket.

'Sorry.' Addie stared down at her boots.

'It's OK,' Gabe said. He pulled his phone from the other pocket. 'It was ages ago. And it was what she wanted anyway.'

'What d'you mean?' Addie said. 'Was she sick, or something?'

'Kind of,' Gabe said. She died the day after my grandad's funeral. Just ran herself a nice warm bubble bath and never got out.' He smiled softly, as if remembering something. 'Married for sixty years, they were,' he said. 'Never apart. Not even for a day.'

Addie stared at him, unsure what to say.

'Come on, you,' Gabe said. 'Time's ticking on. You'd better get cleaned up. Ma won't want Penny to find you smelling of horse poo and covered in straw. It looks bad.'

'Dunno,' Addie said. She scuffed her foot among the straw. 'When I'm ready, all right?' She had waited and waited for Penny. Now she wasn't sure that her legs were going to work properly.

Gabe swept his hair out of his eyes. 'Tell Ma that then, shall I?'

Addie looked up at him. 'Sorry. It's just . . .' She bit her lip.

'I get it,' Gabe said.

He didn't, Addie thought. How could he?

She picked up the foal's bottle and stood it in the bucket. The foal stretched forward hopefully.

'Nothing left,' Addie said. 'Sorry.' She scratched him between his ears.

'Amazing, those ears,' Gabe said.

Addie looked at them. Short, fuzzy. Funny little ears.

Gabe squatted down, as close as he dared to the foal. 'They're short and they sort of fold inwards with just a really narrow opening. See?' He pointed. The foal flinched.

Addie nodded. 'So?'

'Evolution and all that,' Gabe said. 'Ears perfectly shaped for moorland environment: to stop rain and wind, dust and stuff from getting in. One of the reasons these ponies have survived for so long on the moors, so they say. It gets pretty wild out there.'

He raised both eyebrows, smiled. 'As you know.'

'But how . . .?'

Gabe stood up. 'Lesson over for today. Time to go.'

Addie turned away from him. 'She keeps lying,' she said. 'Penny.'

Addie's words were thick and solid in her throat. She buried her face in the foal's soft fur.

'Give her a chance,' Gabe said. He put a hand on her shoulder. The foal eyed him warily. 'See what she says, yeah?'

'Suppose.' Addie sniffed, stood up and brushed herself off.

The foal dug at the straw with one foot, nudged her hip.

'I'll be back soon,' she said. 'I promise.' She followed Gabe outside. Wind blew in her face. It threw back the hood of her coat, hurled bullets of hail that pelted her skin and made small craters in the snow.

'Just a minute,' she said, as Gabe began to close the barn door. She slid back inside. 'Don't be scared,' she whispered to the foal. 'Everything's going to be fine.'

THIRTEEN

'Want to borrow my hat?' Gabe yelled, as they walked back across the yard.

'You're all right,' Addie said. She bent her head against the icy blasts, tugged her hood back in place, held on to it with one hand. This was mean weather, she thought. Mean and angry: worse than the glistening stillness that had come before.

Grey slush had built up near the farmhouse door since Addie had left earlier. Gabe kicked at it, then cleared it away with the snow spade Sam kept under the porch.

'What's the betting your Penny will be wearing her high heels again in this weather?' Gabe said. He grinned. 'Better make a way through for her, just in case.'

'She's not *my* Penny,' Addie said. But the image of Penny in her bright red stilettos, tottering and sliding in the slush, loosened the band that had crept round her stomach. Just a little.

Addie stood on one leg in the hall and struggled to get out of her boots. They seemed frozen to her feet. Her fingers were too stiff with cold to be of any help in pulling them free. It might be raining instead of snowing, but it wasn't getting any warmer on the farm.

Gabe pointed to a wooden settle. 'Sit here,' he said. He swept a pile of scarves, hats and newspapers to one side.

Addie sat. Gabe knelt down and tugged at her right boot. It came quickly free.

Addie looked down at his bowed head, his unruly red hair.

'Did *she* have red hair? Your nan?' she asked.

The second boot came free. Gabe stood it on the mat.

'Nah, hers was grey.' He straightened up, grinned at her, brushed mud from his jeans.

'Funny,' Addie said. 'Only you don't look much like your mam.' She thought of Sam, his coal black eyebrows, the dark fuzz on his close-shaved head. 'Or your dad.'

'I look like my birth dad,' Gabe said. 'Far as I can tell from the rubbish photo I've got . . .'

Addie stared at him. 'What?'

'I'm adopted, Addie. Thought you knew.' He charged

down the hall towards the kitchen. 'Come on. I'm getting a few scones down my neck before Jude's social worker gets near them. He's built like Mountain Man, that Tim. He'll scoff the lot.'

Gabe disappeared round the kitchen door. Addie stared after him. Gabe? Adopted? Gabe, who was as much a part of things here as the smell of wood smoke and the big, wide sky. Gabe, who had Ruth's softness in his eyes and Sam's easy stride.

Questions tumbled around in Addie's head. Her stomach rumbled. Perhaps she'd go and rescue a scone from Gabe; see if he felt like talking some more.

As she washed her hands in the cloakroom, she heard the clink of the yard gate.

They were here.

She wasn't hungry any more.

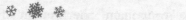

Penny was in the snug, beside the fire. She looked like someone else. Someone smaller than Penny. She had a towel round her shoulders, her hair was flat to her head and there were black mascara stripes on her cheeks. Her jacket was draped over the fireguard to dry. There was no sign of the red stilettos.

She smiled at Addie through a mouthful of scone. Her smile was different too. More of a straight line. It didn't reach her eyes.

'Sorry I was late,' Penny said. 'It's a bit wild out there.' She pushed at her damp hair. 'Even just getting in from the car.'

Addie nodded. The wind hurled rain and hail against the window; rattled the panes as if it wanted to get into the room. A red flame jumped in the hearth.

'It's good to see you, Addie. Are you going to come and sit down?' Penny moved her briefcase from the cushion next to her and put it on the floor alongside the sofa. Next to a case. A green case with a purple ribbon tied to the zip.

The wind was inside Addie's head now. It pounded and whooshed between her ears.

'You've got Mam's case,' she said. 'Is she home then?'

'I'm afraid not, Addie. Not yet.' Penny pulled the case forward. 'I've brought some more of your things for now. Like I said on the phone.' She smiled her new smile again. 'This was the only proper case I could find.' Her mouth twisted at one side. 'I had to put the rest in a bag, I'm afraid.' She leaned round, lifted something heavy from behind Mam's case. 'I apologise.'

A black bag. A black *bin* bag, streaked with rain. Addie could see Mam's pencil box through a hole in the side. She knelt down and pulled it free. A red shirt sleeve came with it, its buttonhole caught in the lid.

'I don't wear this shirt any more,' Addie said. 'I grew out of it ages ago.'

'I'm sorry, Addie. It was hard to know what to bring,' Penny said. 'I couldn't find very much in your room. But don't worry. Ruth will get you a few new things. And you'll have pocket money while you're here. You can spend that however you like.'

The wind roared louder, whipped the flames up the chimney. Words wedged in Addie's throat, hard and dry like the toast at breakfast.

'Addie.' Penny was standing now; moving closer to her. She smelled of rain. Her perfume hurt Addie's nose. 'Come and sit down, sweetheart,' she said.

'You told me Mam was doing OK.' Addie's voice cracked. The fire was behind her eyes now, burning.

Penny perched on the arm of the sofa. 'It's time to be really honest with each other, Addie.' She scrunched her eyebrows together. 'Your mam's not been able to look after you properly for quite a while now, has she?' She swallowed, like the words were too big for *her* mouth too. She brushed a strand of hair from Addie's forehead. Like Mam used to do. 'I couldn't let that go on. It's my job to keep you safe.'

Addie leaned away. 'No,' she said. 'It's not.'

Penny sat up straight. 'It's going to take time for your mum to get well, Addie,' she said. 'Quite a bit of time. She needs to go to that special place I told you about: Riverside, remember?' She peered into Addie's face. Her pupils moved from left to right, right to left, like she was searching for something. Something she couldn't find.

'*I* can look after her,' Addie said. 'I do. When people let me.'

Penny sighed. She scrunched her eyebrows together then lifted them high. 'I know, Addie, sweetheart,' she said. 'But it's your mam's job to take care of *you*, not the other way around. And now there are lots of people trying to help her get better, so that she can. OK?'

'She'll be missing me *so* much,' Addie said. Her heartbeat was in her throat, getting in the way of her words. They came out in a whisper like when she had tonsillitis. Penny's face seemed to be underwater. 'Does she even know where I am?' Addie's bottom lip trembled. She bit into it. Hard.

'It's all right to cry, Addie,' Penny said. 'It will help.'

Addie bit down harder; tasted blood, salty and metallic, on her tongue. She wouldn't cry. Especially not in front of Penny.

Penny took a pack of tissues from her case and held one out to Addie. 'Your mum knows you're here, in foster care, Addie. She signed the papers for you to stay. For now.'

Addie shook her head. 'She wouldn't,' she said. 'She didn't. She needs me.' Addie tore at the tissue and threw it into the air. It fluttered and flapped; fell to the floor like an injured bird.

'She knew she had to, Addie. For your sake. And for her own. She needs to know you're safe while she concentrates on getting better. She did the right thing. The only thing she *can* do. She loves you.'

Penny's phone rang in her bag, its loud, happy ringtone an explosion in Addie's ears.

'Sorry,' Penny said. She pulled the phone from her bag and pressed at it with her blood-red nails.

'When can I visit her?' Addie said. 'When are you taking me?'

The room fell silent, the windowpanes suddenly still, as if even the wind was holding its breath.

'You know, Addie, your mum needs a bit of time first, before you see her. I realise that's very hard for you. But I'll make sure she knows you're OK. Don't worry.'

There it was again. That stupid thing people kept saying. Addie wasn't OK. How could she be?

'I can ring Mam, then. Give me the phone number.'

'Soon, Addie. When she's ready. Not just yet.' Penny glanced at the door, as if hoping it might open. 'Shall we see if Ruth can join us now?' she said.

As if on cue, Ruth's head appeared round the door.

'Ruth, come on in,' Penny said. She patted the seat next to her on the sofa, as if this was her home and Ruth the visitor.

'Are you all right, Addie?' Ruth said. Her kind eyes connected with Addie's. Addie bit her lip again and looked away.

'I know this is tough,' Ruth said. 'Of course it is. But all of us are here for you, Addie. We'll help you get through. And you can help that little foal to do the same, can't you?'

'Yes, Addie, I hear you're a horse whisperer in the making,' Penny said, her voice brighter, as if she was relieved at the change of subject. She folded her hands in her lap; beamed at Addie. 'Tell me about him. It *is* a "him", isn't it? Have you given him a name yet?'

Addie stared at her. 'You said I wasn't allowed to miss any more school,' she said. 'You said it's the law and Mam was breaking it when she didn't make me go!'

'Yes,' Penny said. 'That's right, Addie.' She picked up her cup, realised it was empty, put it back down. 'We do need to get you back to school. And think it will help you – making new friends, having new things to think about.' She glanced at Ruth. 'Any news on this?' she asked.

Addie looked from Penny to Ruth and back again. Something cold crawled on her neck.

'I've already got friends at school,' she said.

She didn't. Not really. Not since Hattie dumped her. Sophie Ward *said* she'd be her friend. But she got fed up because Addie was always away and made friends with Darren Oates' sister instead. She didn't even talk to Addie now; not even if she saw her in the street.

'The thing is, Addie,' Penny said. 'Gas Street School is too far away, isn't it? So we're trying to get you into one round here for now.' Her face brightened. 'In fact, I'm trying to sort out a place for you at the school where Sunni goes. Might not happen until after Easter, though.' She looked up at Ruth, her eyebrows raised.

Ruth nodded. 'Yes, they're full for now.' She smiled at Addie. 'It's too popular. No one wants to leave!'

Penny nodded. 'So Ruth's going to give you some lessons at home until there's a space, fill you in on what you've missed. She used to be a teacher, Addie. Did she say? It'll be fun. And you'll have Jude for company soon. He needs to catch up too.'

Addie turned her back on Penny. It was only February. Easter was ages away. 'Tell Sunni's school I won't need a place,' she said to Ruth. 'Mam'll be better ages before Easter.'

Penny picked up her bag and snapped it shut. 'Just let lovely Ruth and Sam take care of you for a bit, Addie. And no more running off by yourself,' she said. 'Promise me, now.'

Addie stared out from somewhere behind her eyes. She might have nodded. She wasn't sure. If she did, she was lying.

FOURTEEN

Addie locked the bathroom door. She sat on the floor, pulled her knees up under her chin, tucked her head low and tried to disappear.

Voices drifted up the stairs – Ruth, Penny, Sam. Deep, sing-song tones that must belong to Tim. Jude screamed. Flo barked. Something clattered to the floor.

The front door opened and closed, opened and closed. Addie's chest pounded in strange jumps. Perhaps her heart was broken, and she was going to die, right there in the bathroom. Like Luke's nan, who went to be with her husband because she didn't know how to stay in the world without him.

Ruth tapped on the door. She called Addie's name; asked if it was all right to come in. It wasn't. Addie pushed her kneecaps into her eyes – hard, so that it hurt.

Ruth knocked again. Twice. She told Addie it was OK to come down whenever she was ready. She said she was right there if Addie needed her. Her voice was warm and soft and kind. Her footsteps moved away from the door. Stopped. Started again. She was gone.

Addie put her hands over her ears and squeezed away the fire behind her eyes. She didn't need Ruth. She would never need Ruth. She needed Mam. When would she see her again?

She couldn't stay at the farm for weeks and weeks; couldn't start at Sunni's stupid school where everyone would hate her anyway. She wouldn't be the same Addie any more: the Addie from the brown house in the brown street with Mr Borovski's shop on the corner.

Mam would think she didn't love her any more.

She kept forgetting how to breathe. Her breath felt muddled up in her chest and she had to start counting: in, out, in, out, like they did on the hospital programme she used to watch with Mam. Before the telly got taken away.

She didn't want to be by herself in the cold bathroom any more. She turned the big silver key and opened the door.

Flo was lying outside, her black nose resting on her white paws. Her tail thumped on the floor as Addie came out on to the landing. She jumped up and ran to the top of the stairs, her amber eyes turned towards Addie like spotlights.

'I'm coming,' Addie said. 'I'm coming.'

She followed Flo down the stairs. Addie's whole body hurt, as if she'd been crushed under the old tractor out in the yard.

Flo nudged open the door to the kitchen and ran in. Addie hovered in the doorway.

There was only Gabe, bent over his phone in the chair by the fire. Flo settled down beside him, rested her head on his foot.

The kitchen was warm but Addie felt frozen. She went inside.

Clay animals were lined up on the table. Most of them were ponies, Addie could tell. Others were probably pigs. Or sheep. One was definitely an elephant. She picked it up. Its trunk fell off.

Gabe looked up from his phone. 'You're in for it now,' he said. He drew a finger across his neck. 'Sunni made that one.'

Addie shrugged.

Gabe got up from the rocking chair and slammed his phone down on the table. 'Don't know why I've got this thing. Never any signal out here,' he said. He picked up the elephant, pressed the trunk back into place, and held it out for inspection. 'More like a rhinoceros now. Oh well, I *tried* to save you.'

Addie turned away and flopped on to the window seat. Widget curled round her legs. She pulled him on to her lap, hugged him to her chest. She must have squeezed him too hard, because he yowled and jumped down again. 'Sorry, Widget,' she said. She patted her knee. 'Please come back. I'll be gentle.'

Widget glanced over his shoulder at Addie, gave one flick of his tail, and climbed into his basket by the stove.

Addie sighed. She wanted to feel his sleepy warmth, hear his reassuring purr.

'You OK?' Gabe asked. 'If you need Ma, she's just nipped out to the barn. She won't be long.'

Addie inspected the skin on her thumb. It was red and sore round the edge of the nail. She chewed at it. 'Where's Jude?' she said.

'Sunni's taken him for a bit of fresh air. He was pretty upset. Something Tim said.'

'Like Sunni's going to cheer him up.'

Gabe smiled. 'She's a good kid, Addie. She just gets scared sometimes.'

'She's not *scared*. She's just spiteful. And rude.'

89

'She's scared. Of you, Addie: worried you're gonna steal her spotlight.' Gabe went to the fridge and peered inside. 'Like I was when *she* came.' He brought a slab of cheese to the table and hacked at it with a knife.

'When, Gabe?' she said. 'When did you come here?'

'When I was two.' Gabe shook his head. 'Man, you should see the photos! You think that foal's cute!' He shoved a huge chunk of cheese into his mouth. His cheeks bulged as he chewed.

'But why don't you live with your real parents?' Addie said.

Gabe swallowed, wiped the back of his hand across his mouth. 'I *do*, Addie,' he said. 'And they're the best.' He patted his stomach. 'Definitely room in here for another of those excellent scones. Any idea where Ma's hidden them?' He jumped from his chair and disappeared inside the pantry, humming another of his crazy tunes.

Addie chewed at her bottom lip. She tried to make sense of what Gabe had said. Maybe he just didn't want to talk about his real parents.

Or maybe he'd forgotten them.

Well, she could never, *ever* forget about Mam.

She went across to the table, sat down. She separated

the clay ponies from the other animals that Sunni had made. She stood the two smallest ones together, grouped the big ones around them in a tight circle. 'There you go,' she whispered. 'You're all together again now. A proper family.'

Gabe reappeared with a packet of chocolate finger biscuits. 'Either Ma's got clever with her hiding places, or I was right about Tim,' he said. 'Not a scone in sight.' He sat down next to Addie; grinned.

'When is the foal going back to *his* family?' Addie said.

Gabe chewed; swallowed. 'Difficult one,' he said.

'Why?'

'Well, for a start, we don't know where he's from yet. Which herd.'

Addie looked at the group of clay ponies, nose to tail on the table. '*He* knows,' Addie said. 'He could find them; find his mam. If you took him to the moor.'

Gabe shook his head. 'Not that simple,' he said. 'He belongs to someone. All the wild ponies do. Only he's a late-born, so he got missed in the autumn round-ups. Must've wandered off.'

'Round-ups?'

'Yeah. Each year's foals are rounded up before the

winter sets in. Your little guy shouldn't have been out there by himself. Not in all this.' He waved his arm towards the window. 'It's not done him much good.'

'He's getting stronger already,' Addie said. 'So, when he's better . . .'

'There are rules, Addie. Whoever owns the herd he's from gets to say where he goes. It's weird, though, cos Sam's already phoned round a bit and, so far, none of the owners has a mare missing, or a mare without her foal. But they'll have a better idea once they've seen our little guy. Then they'll decide what to do.'

'When? When will they come?'

'When he's a bit older. Couple of months on, when his proper coat starts to show. But, most likely, they won't put him back out on the moor, anyway.'

Addie stared at Gabe. A gust of hail hit the window.

Gabe held his biscuit in mid-air. 'Sam did tell you that, didn't he?'

Addie shook her head. 'But why?' she said. 'That's just cruel.'

'It's complicated, Addie.' Gabe looked up into the air, as if he was searching for his words there. 'It's to do with making sure that only the right babies get born. Only the pure-bloods. We don't know if this foal is one of those.'

'What does "pure-blood" mean?' Addie asked. And how could it matter, anyway? she thought.

'It means that both his parents have to be proper Exmoor ponies,' Gabe explained. 'Then he'll be one, too, and not –'

'He was born on the moor,' Addie said, interrupting him. 'So of course he's an Exmoor pony.'

Gabe took a bite of biscuit, chewed it slowly; swallowed. He shook his head. 'No, not necessarily,' he said. 'Every now and again a Dartmoor pony finds its way on to Exmoor – I can show you where that is on Dad's map, if you like. It's quite a way for them, but they manage it sometimes.'

Addie shook her head. She didn't care about Dartmoor. Didn't care *where* the foal's parents came from.

'So, one of his parents might be a stray Dartmoor,' Gabe went on. 'The experts can do a blood test to check, if they're not sure, when the foal gets to about six months old. But even if he turns out to be a "pure-blood" Exmoor, he might get sold anyway. Boy foals often do, Dad says. Some for showing, if they look the way they should, but most get bought as riding ponies, or go to a sort of rescue centre, I think.'

'Well, our foal *has* to go back where he came from,' Addie said. 'He *needs* to.' The clay models wavered in front of her; their colours blurred and swam together. She stood up. Her chair scraped on the tiled floor. Flo sprang to her feet, eyes alert.

'You can't keep him away from his family just because of some stupid people and their stupid rules!'

'Whoa.' Gabe held up his hands. 'Don't shoot the messenger.' His eyes caught Addie's. 'Not good news today then? About your mum?'

Addie opened her mouth; closed it. She flicked crumbs from the table.

She felt Gabe's eyes move away.

'Anyway, like I said, it's complicated with the foal.' Gabe swept his fingers through his hair. 'Best ask Dad,' he said. 'But those "stupid rules" – they're there for the best. To do with conservation of the species and everything.'

'For the best?' Addie snatched the biscuit from Gabe's hand and threw it on to the floor. Flo dived to collect it. 'How can it be "for the best" to stop the foal from going home?'

Addie clenched her fists, dug her nails into the soft skin of her palms. She jumped to her feet. 'You're just like Penny,' she shouted. 'Deciding things. Thinking you know best. Well, you don't. You're all just mean, mean, mean. And horrible.' She glared at Gabe. '*All* of you.'

Ruth's best blue plates rattled on the dresser as Addie yanked the door open and charged into the hall. Fire fizzed in her arms and legs. She wanted to kick out like the foal. To run.

Jude was sitting at the bottom of the stairs, still wearing one of his green frog wellies. His usually pale cheeks were red and blotchy. His shoulders shook. He glanced up at her, his eyes wide; afraid.

What had happened with Tim?

Where was Sunni?

Addie took a deep breath. She sat down beside Jude and tried to be still.

'Ruth's coming,' she said. 'She won't be long.'

FIFTEEN

'Maybe your foal would like to meet Jude this morning,' Ruth said. 'What do you think, Addie?' She cleared Addie and Jude's untouched porridge bowls on to the worktop and sat down at the table next to Jude. His chair screeched on the tiles as he wriggled it away from her.

Addie looked at Ruth. There was a small line between her eyebrows. Like an exclamation mark. Addie hadn't noticed it before.

'Don't know,' she said. She glanced at Jude. 'The foal's still really scared.'

Jude lifted his head, turned to Addie. His face was paler than ever, the shadows beneath his eyes deeper; darker. He hadn't slept either, then.

Addie had heard him whimpering through the night. She had pulled her pillow over her ears to stop Jude's sadness from creeping into her head next to her own. There wasn't any room left.

'OK,' she said. 'I suppose. If he wants to.'

'He does,' Sunni said.

Jude got down from his seat; stood next to it, stiff and still.

'Told you,' Sunni said. She scraped her spoon around her bowl. 'Me too,' she said, through her last mouthful of porridge. 'Only later. I'm helping Gabe, learning to work Flo.' She stuck her chin in the air. 'Gabe says I'm born to be a shepherd.'

Addie thought of Sunni's delicate dresses; her silver bangles and polished hair. Her sharp voice and bossy ways. She couldn't see her having anything to do with cold fields or the nervous, runaway sheep that Gabe talked about.

And the foal wouldn't like her, anyway.

'Come on, Jude,' Addie said. 'The foal's waiting for his breakfast.'

'Hats, coats and scarves,' Ruth said. She smiled at Addie, mouthed a thank-you. 'Both of you, now.'

Jude pushed his arms into the sleeves of his duffel coat, very slowly, as if there might be something inside that would bite him. He swung away from Addie when she tried to help him with the stiff toggles. He refused to put on his boots until Addie opened the door, then he stood on the outside mat and pushed his feet into them.

His toes pointed in opposite directions. He took the boots off, inspected them; put them back on the right way round.

Addie stifled a sigh. He was taking forever. She leaned against the wall. Waited.

The air smelled clean. Icicles hung like silver swords from the edges of the porch. Addie reached towards one of them. A shiver of crystal water ran down her wrist and under the sleeve of her coat.

A small brown bird hopped across the yard in the direction of the barn. It left a trail of tiny forked footprints in the snow.

'Look, Jude,' Addie said. 'Let's follow the bird. Come on.'

Jude stuffed both hands into his pockets and shuffled after Addie. The bird hopped ahead of them, then flew on to a stone mounting block by the barn, its breast a tiny red flag to mark the spot. A robin. It stared at her, tilted its head to one side. It looked friendly. Nothing like the scrawny sparrows that picked over chip papers and Coke cans on the common behind Addie's house.

The robin spread its wings and took off as Addie and Jude came close. It perched on Sam's old tractor for a moment and was gone.

'Follow me inside, Jude,' Addie said. 'Slowly, OK?' The warning wasn't really needed, she thought. Jude did everything slowly. Except eating.

She pressed her shoulder against the barn door, eased it open a little. She heard the scrape of the foal's hooves as he got to his feet inside his pen.

Jude shook his head.

Addie reached a hand towards him. 'It's all right. Come on.'

Jude pointed away from the barn, towards the fields beyond the stone wall that edged the yard.

'What is it, Jude? We have to feed the foal. He's waiting for us.'

Jude pointed again. He jabbed furiously into the air, in the direction of the fields beyond the barn. His eyes widened, pressed into Addie's as if to tell her something important.

'What, Jude? What?'

Jude turned and ran behind the barn. Addie stared after him.

Jude. Running. She hadn't seen *that* before.

'Jude!' she shouted.

Where was he going? He wasn't allowed to go off on his own. Addie looked back at the barn door; listened.

The foal would wonder why she hadn't come to him. But she had to go and see what Jude was up to.

He was waiting by a narrow gate that led from the yard into fields and meadows beyond. He opened it, slid through to the other side, and beckoned for Addie to follow him.

He flapped his arms, hopped from one foot to the other. What was he trying to say?

He took off across the field.

The ground was rutted and slippery with partly melted snow and ice. Addie struggled to keep her balance as she hurried after Jude. How come he was managing to move so quickly for once? She caught up with him as he climbed over a small stile. He lost his footing and slid to the ground on his bottom among a green-brown sludge of muddy snow.

Addie jumped down next to him. 'What're you doing?' she said. 'You can't just run off.'

Jude inspected his hands, brushed them together. His nose wrinkled. Red spots appeared on both his cheeks. He rubbed at the stains on his jeans. His mouth opened wide; closed again. His breath escaped in ragged white puffs.

'You're all right,' Addie said. What would she do if he

had one of his meltdowns out here? She shouldn't have agreed to take him to see the foal; she should have asked Ruth to bring him herself.

Jude took a deep breath in. Then another. He got to his feet. He pointed ahead with a mud-stained finger. Addie followed his gaze.

In one corner of the field, a great oak tree dwarfed everything around it. The trunk was divided, riven almost in two for several feet upwards, so that the tree seemed to straddle the ground with giant legs. Bare branches clutched at the sky like the claws of some long-dead creature. Jude slowed down and walked towards it. He kept checking back to see that Addie was following. He picked his way over great roots that poked through the snow, steadying himself with one hand against the vast trunk.

Addie stumbled, looked down to see where to tread safely. When she looked up, Jude was nowhere to be seen.

Her feet slipped and twisted between the roots. She trailed a hand against the tree for balance, as Jude had done. The bark was rough and cold, pitted with knots and craters.

She peered into the dark belly of the ruined oak.

Jude's face loomed from the musty blackness, pale as the moon. His white hands lifted and fell like wings.

A yellow beam blinded Addie. She stepped back. The beam of light waved up and down, then flicked off. On. Off again.

Torchlight. Jude had a torch.

'Where'd that come from?' Addie said.

Jude emerged and stood beside Addie. He directed the torch beam inside the hollow. It split and danced in the darkness. Specks of light flitted like a thousand fireflies in the black space. Addie was blinded by their frantic spin.

She rubbed her eyes, turned to look at Jude. His shape was hazy against the daylight outside the tree.

'What *is* that?' she whispered.

Jude moved past her, fiddling with the torch. The beam narrowed, became weaker. The fireflies stilled, glimmered like minute stars in the gloom. Addie blinked; closed her eyes. Sparks of colour still danced inside them. She waited a moment, then moved further inside the cavern.

The now pale torchlight slid across the walls. They were draped with fabric. Peacock blue, vibrant greens and golds swirled across the surface; tiny round mirrors caught the light, glinted among the folds. Sunni's sari fabric. From her special box.

'Sunni?' Addie said. 'Sunni did this?'

Jude nodded.

Addie looked back over her shoulder.

'She won't like us being here,' she said.

Jude nudged her elbow. He stared up at her and jabbed at his chest.

'What? Sunni said you could show me?'

Jude shook his head. He jabbed harder, with both hands now. The torchlight whipped across his face. What was he trying to say?

Jude pulled at Addie's sleeve, drew her backwards. He shone the torch to one side of the entrance to the tree room.

Letters. White. Rough. Carved into the ancient bark. Addie followed the beam across them:

Jude
and
thomas
Their place.

'This is yours!' Addie said. 'Sunni did this for *you*?'

Jude nodded. The fireflies were in his eyes now.

Addie traced the words with one finger.

'Thomas. Is that your friend?'

Jude looked away. When he looked back, the fireflies had gone.

He switched off the torch and scrambled back outside.

'Wait, Jude.' Addie followed him into the field.

It was raining again, a wet drizzle that clung to her face like a fine net. The sky was heavy, the early blue vanished and replaced by grey clouds.

Jude wasn't wearing his hat. He must have left it in the tree. Tiny droplets of rain were caught in his hair.

'Put your hood up, Jude,' Addie said. She reached forward and flipped it up on top of his head. Jude flinched; pushed the hood away. He ploughed forward, his head bent low on his chest. Addie wished she hadn't asked about Thomas. But who *was* he?

'You can give the foal his milk, if you like,' she said. 'He usually only lets me, but he'll let you too. I know he will.'

Jude pushed his hands into his pockets. The grey sky filled his eyes.

Addie had made him disappear again.

Addie handed the bottle of milk to Jude. The foal studied him from beneath his long lashes, then moved towards him and began to feed.

'Told you,' Addie said. 'He likes you.'

The foal pulled hard on the rubber teat and dragged it from Jude's grasp. It fell on to the straw. The foal nosed at it; tried to put his lips around the teat again.

'You have to hold it with both hands,' Addie said. 'I'll show you.' She picked up the bottle, held it out to Jude. 'He's getting really strong now. And greedy, too'

Jude shook his head; folded his arms behind his back.

'You've got to,' Addie said. 'I need to go and mix his special cereal for afterwards. He doesn't like waiting. He's only a baby.'

She tucked the bottle between Jude's feet, picked up the foal's feeding bucket and went to the other end of the barn to fill it from the sacks of meal stored in the last pen. She climbed on top of one of them and peered across the pen walls at Jude and the foal.

They stood facing one another. Still. Silent. The foal stepped forward, nuzzled close to Jude's ear, as if whispering to him. Jude stepped back. The foal shook his head, blew down his nose and whinnied softly. Addie saw him stumble a little on his gangly, uncertain legs; heard the scrape of his hooves against the floor. He wanted that milk. She'd better go and see to it herself. She jumped down from the sack of meal, threw handfuls of feed into the bucket and set off back across the barn.

Wind whistled in the rafters above her. Gabe had warned of a storm; said the cows had come out from under the trees to be safe from lightning. They were never wrong, *he* said.

But there was another sound too: gentle, thin. What was it? Addie stopped, put down the bucket, strained to hear between the gusts of wind.

A small voice rose and fell – soft, husky, barely more than a broken whisper.

Jude. It was Jude.

Jude *singing*.

Addie crept towards the stall. The singing stopped.

The foal lay in the straw, legs tucked beneath him. Jude was kneeling beside him, stroking his white muzzle. The empty feeding bottle stood beside him.

Addie held her breath.

'Thomas – has – milk,' Jude said. He jumped, as if startled; glanced up at Addie. His chin trembled. He looked back down at the foal.

Addie breathed out. Her heart beat in her ears. Jude singing. Jude *talking*.

What if she broke the spell? Made Jude's voice go away again?

She knelt down next to him, fondled the foal's velvet ears. 'Is . . . is Thomas a baby too, then?'

Jude nodded.

'What, your baby brother?'

Jude's chin sank on to his chest, as if his head was suddenly too heavy for him. He stared up at Addie. A tear slid from one eye. It clung to his cheek: silver, perfect, clear as melting ice. 'Thomas likes songs,' he said.

'Where *is* Thomas?' Addie said. 'Is he with your mam?'

Jude shook his head, covered his face with his hands.

His sobs echoed around the barn, echoed inside Addie; became part of the rain and the wind. Part of the wildness of winter. Part of the gentle breath of the sleeping foal.

SIXTEEN

Jude slid round the barn door. He turned, pressed both hands against it, and tried to heave it shut. His boots slid backwards on the dusty flagstones. The door groaned, shifted just a little. Jude groaned too and gave up. He sauntered over to Addie, hands in the pockets of his duffel coat.

'Can't do it,' he grunted.

Addie glanced at the partially closed door. A beam of light had followed Jude inside. It stretched like a stage spotlight towards them, warmed Addie's arms.

'It's OK,' she said. 'I needed a bit more light and it's not cold today.'

Addie loved this soft spring light. It made everything on the farm look bright and new, as if the bitter snows had washed the world clean in readiness for better things to come. Tiny new bulbs pushed green shoots through the earth under the hedgerows; delicate snowdrops already showed their brave white flowers.

There were green buds on the trees and shiny yellow cowslips in the fields.

Jude was talking: a little more every day.

Hope blossomed inside Addie. Mam would feel better too, now spring was here. Addie just knew she would.

She turned back to the foal, began moving a wide silver comb through his mane. It caught almost immediately. Addie stopped, gently teased two thick strands of hair from its metal teeth

Jude's small, serious face tilted towards her, still scarlet with effort. 'What's his name?' he asked. His words seemed to echo around the barn. His eyes widened, as if the sound of his voice was as much a surprise for him, as it sometimes still was for Addie.

'He doesn't have a name,' she said. 'He's a wild pony. Wild animals don't have names.'

'Do so.' Jude inspected the straw, scuffed at it with his foot. 'Simba does. An' he's a *lion*.'

The foal shook his head, stretched his neck round and nudged at Addie's arm.

'*And* Sam's cows,' Jude added. He nodded his head emphatically. 'They got names.'

Addie thought of Sam's 'girls': Betsy, Josephine and the rest, with their strange, staring eyes and flared nostrils; their low, eerie calls. 'Cows aren't wild animals, Jude,' she said, not entirely sure that she was right. 'And Simba's made up. In a film. That's different.'

Jude folded his arms across his chest. 'Well, the foal *wants* a name. A special name,' he added, in a whisper.

Addie ran her hand down the foal's nose, felt his leathery lips open and close against her skin. 'You're OK, aren't you, boy?' she said. 'You know who you are.'

She put the comb in her pocket and crouched down in front of Jude.

'We can't give him a name, Jude. He doesn't belong to us. He doesn't belong on a farm with people and cows and snuffling pigs in pens made out of brick. He belongs to his mam. He belongs to the forest and the moor and the big wide sky out there.' She stood up again. 'He's a wild animal, like I said. He doesn't want to stay here, so he doesn't want a name, all right?'

Jude's chin sank. 'Doesn't look wild,' he muttered. He blinked. Once. Twice. Was he going to cry again?

Addie sighed. What was it about Jude that squeezed at her heart like a fist?

'Come on, Jude,' she said. 'You can help me. I'll show you how. You'll be a good hairdresser.' She picked up a flat, round brush. 'Like this. Watch.' She swept the brush in gentle downward strokes over the foal's flanks. 'Don't press too hard.' She held the brush out to Jude.

Jude took it, turned it over in his hands. His shoulders lifted a little.

'And if you *really* want to,' Addie said, 'I suppose *you* could think of a name. Then you could call him that. In your head.'

Jude looked up. Light flickered across his face. His mouth twisted to one side. He brightened, smiled his small smile. 'Feather,' he announced. 'Feather.' He pointed the brush at the narrow patch of white hairs on the foal's forehead. 'Cos he's got one. There.'

Addie traced the shape with her finger. When had it first appeared? It hadn't been there to begin with and now it was. Curled like the feathers that drifted from the henhouse and lifted on the breeze. Snow-white, like the feather that she had once found on her bedroom windowsill at home. An angel had left it there. That's what Mam said. Addie had kept it under her pillow for weeks.

Jude moved closer. The foal nosed at his pocket. 'I don't got sweets today,' he whispered. He glanced over his shoulder at Addie.

'He knows you *have*, though, Jude!' Addie shook her head. There was always something in those pockets, despite Ruth's eagle eyes and a new hiding place for the treats tin in the kitchen.

Jude's cheeks flushed pink. He leaned in, squinted at the foal's head. 'Might *not* be a feather,' he said. 'Might be a snowflake. Is it, Addie?'

Addie shrugged. 'We'll have to wait and see, as he grows.' She thought of those first Exmoor snowflakes again: fragile and gentle on her skin as she set out to escape the farm, to find her way back to Mam. She remembered her desperation; her fear at being separated from Mam for even one more day; her fear of this unfamiliar wild world. She hadn't thought she could survive any of it. But she had. So far.

They had. Addie and the snow foal. Together.

'Snowflake wouldn't be the right name for him, Jude,' she said. 'Snowflakes are delicate. This foal is tough. And strong.' She leaned forward and wrapped her arms round his arched neck. 'And brave. Very, very brave.'

Jude moved away. He dropped the brush on to the straw; stuffed his hands deep into his pockets. He tucked his chin down low, like the shy pigeons in the rafters above his head.

'Aren't you helping then?' Addie said.

'When will I be brave?' he muttered into his coat.

'You already are,' Addie said. 'Every day. Now come on, let's get this little one looking his best. Sam says it's time to take him outside for a bit.'

She took the foal's face between her hands. 'You'll have to be brave all over again when Sam comes,' she said. 'But me and Jude will help you, so you'll be OK.'

The foal stared back at Addie. His eyes still and trusting.

But going outside meant wearing straps round his face, being pulled at; led away on a rein or rope, Gabe had said. What would a wild foal make of all that? Addie wondered.

And what would he make of leaving his soft bed of straw and the safety of the low-lit barn; of the yard with its noisy cobbles, scuttling hens and huge, rusted red tractor?

Addie already knew the answer. But if the foal was ever going to get back to his moorland home, back to *his* mam, he had to cope.

Was there a way to make it easier for him?

She dragged the foal's feed bucket close to his nose and bundled some handfuls of fresh hay into it. 'Come on, Jude,' she said. 'You can do your hairdressing later. I've got an idea.'

✳ ❄ ✳

Addie searched among the coats hanging in the hallway and found her long striped scarf underneath Sam's yellow waterproof jacket. 'Got it,' she said. 'Right, back to the barn, Jude.'

Ruth called from the kitchen, 'Addie. Jude. Come on in now. There's a snack for you. Wash your hands, please.'

Jude stared at Addie. 'I'm hungry,' he said.

Addie sighed. 'OK, but we have to be quick.'

Gabe and Ruth were at the table surrounded by a pile of books.

Gabe looked up. He flopped back in his chair, mopped his brow. 'A rescue party. At last!' he said. He closed the lid of his laptop.

'We're nearly done here,' Ruth said. She ruffled Gabe's hair. 'But not quite.' She opened the laptop again. 'Your turn this afternoon, you two.' She smiled at Addie and Jude. 'We'll make it fun, I promise!'

Jude climbed on to his chair, stared expectantly at Ruth.

'Over on the range, Addie,' Ruth said. She pointed to a tray of golden flapjacks. 'Bring them over, sweetheart.'

They did look good. They smelled wonderful too:

warm and sweet and syrupy. Addie supposed they had time for one. Or two.

Flo hopped out of her basket as Addie carried the tray to the table. She positioned herself beside Gabe and stared her amber stare. She knew better than to waste her time with Jude. When Gabe didn't give in, Flo turned her attention to Addie.

No wonder she could make Sam's sheep do whatever she wanted, Addie thought, as she dropped a chunk of flapjack under the table.

'Flo, basket,' Gabe said. 'Go. No more hypnotising Addie.'

Flo slunk away, dragging the trailing end of Addie's scarf part of the way with her, as if in defiance.

Gabe retrieved it. 'Not cold are you, Addie?' He grinned. 'I'm out there in my T-shirt now the snow's gone.'

'And your hat,' Jude said, through a huge mouthful of food.

'Always.' Gabe nodded. 'You'd look pretty good in a beanie yourself, Jude.' He pulled a purple one from his back pocket. 'Here. Try this'.

Jude shrank away, placed his hands over his head.

'He doesn't want to,' Addie said. 'He doesn't like purple.'

'Quite right.' Gabe whisked the hat away. 'So last season.'

Addie brushed crumbs from her hands. She had important things to do. And less time than she'd thought to do them, now that Ruth was planning school work for after lunch.

'Come on, Jude,' she said. 'You'll burst if you eat any more flapjack.'

Jude prodded at his stomach. 'Won't,' he said. But he wiped his hand across his mouth, slid down from his seat, and went to wash the stickiness from his face and fingers.

Addie noticed that he no longer had to stand on tiptoes to reach the taps. He was growing, just like the foal.

SEVENTEEN

Addie rolled her scarf into a bundle, held it close to the foal's nose. He nudged it. His nostrils opened and closed. He pushed his face against it.

'Good boy,' she said.

'What you doing, Addie?' Jude whispered.

'Shhhh!' Addie looked over her shoulder at him, held a finger to her lips.

She unrolled the scarf, stroked it along the foal's warm cheek and over his forehead. His eyes narrowed a little, as if he might be sleepy. Addie laid the scarf across the base of his neck. He turned and nosed at it; looked at Addie, his head tipped to one side.

'It's OK,' she said. 'You're doing really well.'

'What're you doing, though?' Jude's legs jiggled with impatience.

Addie looped the ends of the scarf together and stepped away. The foal shifted from foot to foot, bent forward and took a long drink from his water trough.

His ears stood straight and stiff, but he lifted his head and stared at Addie, as if asking the same question. Then he was still. So far, so good.

She crossed the fingers of both hands for a moment, then reached for the loop of scarf. She took a step back. And another. The fabric became taught. The foal's head jerked in alarm. He backed towards the rear of the stall, stretching the scarf tighter against his neck.

'Those sweets, Jude,' Addie said, 'in your pocket. Hold one out for him.'

Jude delved into both pockets, brought out a packet of Polo mints and a handful of fruit bonbons welded together in a clump. 'Polos,' he said. 'Polos are his favourite.'

He held out two in an outstretched palm.

'A bit closer,' Addie said.

It worked. The foal sniffed the air, stretched out his neck, took a step forward. Then another. He drew his sweet prize into his mouth, crunched it between his flat teeth.

'Well done,' Addie said. 'Good boy.' She fondled his ears.

'Hold out some more, Jude,' she whispered, 'only this time, don't let him get them so quickly. Just keep moving away. Towards the door. Slowly. Really slowly.'

There was only one mint left by the time they reached the door.

'Open it a bit, Jude,' Addie said. 'Just a *little* bit.'

The foal stopped in his tracks, nostrils flaring at the slow scrape of the door, the influx of light and new smells on the air. He tossed his head, pulled back. Addie felt his hot, panicked breath on her face and hands. He showed no interest in Jude's mints.

'He's scared,' Jude said. 'Don't make him, Addie.'

Addie let the makeshift leading rein fall slack. What should she do now? She thought of Sam, how he calmed his nervous cows with his firm, gentle commands; of Ruth, calming Jude with her stillness, her quiet presence beside him. 'We'll just stay here,' she said. 'Stand with him a bit. Show him *we're* not scared.'

But Addie *was* scared. What should she do now? The scarf idea had come from Gabe: he'd told her how he'd used his own to start training Flo when she was a puppy; how animals are comforted by the scent of the person that they trust. This scarf smelled of Addie. That had been enough for the foal. Until now. Now she was asking him to do something much more frightening. Should she leave going outside until

119

another day, or would that make his fear worse?

And what if they did manage to get him outside and then he really panicked? What would they do then?

Jude leaned in, cupped his hand round Addie's ear. 'I know a good idea,' he whispered. 'I seen it in a film. A cowboy one. We got to cover his eyes up.'

Addie chewed her lip. She'd seen a film like that too; she'd watched it with Mam. She remembered terrified horses in a burning barn; the crackle and leap of flames around them; the thick smoke. Two women had thrown blankets over their heads to still their panic and led them all to safety. But that was all just made up. Not real. And Addie didn't have a blanket, only her stripy scarf. Could that work, with a real pony?

Maybe it was worth a try. She didn't have any other ideas.

Addie stared into the foal's eyes and slowly moved the scarf until both were covered, tied it behind his ears. She pressed her forehead against his, smoothed his neck with both hands. She felt him relax a little. Tears prickled behind her eyes. She waited a minute or two, then inched her way through the doorway, hardly daring to breathe.

The foal followed.

Addie glanced at Jude. His chin was held high.

Out in the yard, sensing the open space around him, the foal froze again. But there was no backing away, no rearing high like the terrified horses in the Wild West barns, just sweat glistening on his skin, a trembling in his long limbs.

Addie rested her hand lightly on the foal's back, to let him know that she was beside him. She felt his racing heart, the twitch of muscles, the quick breaths. She waited.

Jude's curls lifted and twisted in the breeze. Otherwise, he too was still. Addie closed her own eyes, watched the drift of colour and light behind her lids. Was that what the foal was seeing? She wished she knew.

They might have stood there for ten minutes or an hour; Addie couldn't tell. But, eventually, she felt the soft fuzz of the foal's muzzle against her neck. She opened her eyes and hugged him close.

Jude was sitting on the mounting block, a small statue by the barn door. 'We did it,' he said.

Addie nodded. '*He* did it,' she said. 'With your help.' She kissed the foal's forehead. She made soft, crooning sounds that she knew from somewhere long forgotten. She eased his blindfold, lifted the edge. Just a little. She tried to keep her own breathing steady and soft. She slipped the scarf down over the foal's ears and knotted it round his neck, like before.

His head swung from side to side. He lifted it, stared up into the sky. He whinnied softly.

'Well done, boy,' Addie said. 'And well done, Jude.'

She was suddenly exhausted. And starving.

'That's enough for today,' she said to the foal. 'Let's get you back inside for some lunch and a good rest.'

As she settled him in his stall, Addie wondered what Ruth and Sam would say when they heard what she and Jude done. She might be in trouble. It didn't matter. After today, Gabe and Sam could come with their straps and buckles and their leather reins. The foal would manage just fine – wouldn't he? Just as long as Addie was there beside him.

After today, he was one step closer to being back with his mam.

And Addie would be seeing her own mam before long – Penny had promised. She might even have rung with the arrangements while Addie had been busy in the barn.

Addie smiled. She would soon be home too.

She put her arm round Jude's shoulders as they

walked back to the farmhouse, stomachs rumbling in unison. He let it stay there for a moment before shrugging it away.

EIGHTEEN

Addie slid the leather halter over the foal's head and fastened the buckle at the side. It was easier now that he had shed most of his shaggy winter coat. Easier now that he was no longer afraid of the clips and straps round his face and neck. She ran her fingers under the cheek straps to make sure they weren't too tight, like Gabe and Sam had taught her. She was a quick learner, Sam had said.

And so was the foal. He stood still, let Addie finish, then scraped at the straw with his front hoof.

'You know what this halter means now, don't you?' She stroked his nose. 'Adventure! Good boy,' she said. 'Let's go and find Jude.'

The foal trotted behind her across the yard, his feet sure now on the cobbles. He stopped when Addie tried to lead him past the tractor, as he always did; pulled back on the leading rein. His eyes sought Addie's for reassurance. Addie waited, spoke softly in his ear.

The fuzz of fur that edged it tickled her nose.

The foal trotted on. His steps quickened as Addie led him from the yard and on to the narrow path through Sam's hayfield. His ears swivelled at the sounds of the spring morning: the twitter of birds in the hedgerows, the deep call of sheep in the distance, the thin answering bleat of their new lambs. He strained ahead as they came close to the meadow, lowered his head and nudged at the gate.

'Hold on,' Addie said. She unlatched the gate, closed it carefully behind her and set the foal free from the rein.

He didn't move to begin with, but lifted his head; sniffed the air. He kicked his heels, skipped and danced among the rough grass and white clover. He galloped in a circle. He lay down and rolled on his back. His long legs wriggled in the air.

Addie laughed; wondered how it might feel to skip and roll on the grass like the foal.

He's so happy out here, she thought. *Happy to be free.* He had never belonged in the windowless barn. He belonged out here, under the wide sky with the wind ruffling his mane, and the trees waving above him.

He belonged with his mother.

Jude was kneeling under his oak tree at the far end of the meadow, counting the pale primroses that had sprouted between the roots. They swayed in the breeze like small yellow butterflies. They were Jude's pride and joy.

Mam would love them, too, Addie knew. She would take her sketch pad from her bag and she would draw them; she would capture them with her pen, paper and paint.

Well, soon she would come and see them for herself.

Addie sat down on one of the oak's big roots, resting her chin on her knees. The foal wandered nearby and nibbled at the grass.

'D'you think the foal still remembers his mother, Jude?' she said. 'You know, still misses her?'

Jude looked up from his counting. He frowned. 'Now I forgot,' he said. He crawled back to where he had started and began to count again.

Addie waited. The sun was warm, gentle. She unzipped her jacket, knelt down next to Jude and turned her face to the sky. It was a pale grey-blue. What would Mam call it? Eggshell. Eggshell blue. That was it.

She looked up into the spread of branches above; at the dark, empty nests balanced there. Sunni had said birds would find them soon and lay their eggs in them; make new families. When would they come?

Jude finished counting and shuffled closer to Addie.

'What's ten add eleven?' he said. He spread his fingers wide, stared at them as if there might be some missing. Fragments of bark and soil clung to his palms. He didn't seem to have noticed.

'Twenty-one,' Addie said.

'Twenty-one flowers,' Jude said. He nodded. 'That makes . . .' He held up his fingers again, trapped the little finger of each hand beneath his thumbs. 'Six new ones.' He folded his arms across his chest. 'Sam says there never were so much as there is this year.'

'Many . . .' Addie said. 'There were never so many.'

Jude's mouth twisted to one side. 'Anyway,' he said, 'Sam said it's cos I look after them so good.'

Addie smiled at him. 'Brilliant, Jude,' she said. 'Well done.'

Jude stood up. The foal trotted towards him, nuzzled his side. Jude pulled something from his pocket and held it in his palm under the foal's nose. The foal took it, crunched it between his teeth.

'Not sugar lumps, again, Jude?' Addie said. 'They're bad for him. I told you.'

Jude shrugged. 'My dad gave *me* some,' Jude said. 'If I was good.' He stroked the foal's nose, pressed his cheek against it. 'And he *is* good, aren't you, foal?'

Addie smiled and shook her head. 'No more, though, Jude. And no more Polos either. Except in emergencies. His lovely new teeth might fall out. We have to give him carrot or apple instead now.'

Jude fingered the gap in his own teeth. 'Why did his mam leave him – all by his self?' he said.

'Don't know. I told you.' Addie twisted her fingers in the grass. 'Sam says he just got missed somehow in the winter round-up,' she said. 'And that his mam might've got sick, you know, before that . . .' She pictured the foal huddled against his mother's side on the winter moor, wondering when she would wake up. 'He must've been so cold and hungry,' she said. 'And *really, really* scared.'

'Why didn't nobody look for him, though?' Jude asked.

'It's like Sam said, Jude. Remember? None of the herd owners knew about him.'

'Only his mam did.'

'Yes. And the other ponies.'

'Maybe they all forgot him now,' Jude said. 'Now they didn't see him for a long time.' He took the foal's face in his hands and stared into his eyes. 'He didn't forget *them*, though.' He looked up at Addie. 'If he's got a brother,' he said, 'he'll remember him forever 'n' ever.' He buried his head in the foal's neck.

Addie's throat felt tight. 'Of course he'll remember him,' she said. She reached towards him and let her hand brush his arm. 'You'll see Thomas soon, Jude. Tim said, didn't he?'

Jude looked up, gave a quick nod. He stared into the distance for a long moment. Addie saw that he was somewhere else – remembering. She waited.

He sniffed loudly, wiped his nose on his sleeve and got to his feet. He clambered slowly across the roots of the oak and collected the watering can Sam had given him. He clutched it with both hands, held it high underneath his chin, stumbled back towards Addie.

'I'm strong now,' he said, grimacing with the effort. He thumped the watering can on to the ground beside her. Water jumped from the nozzle. 'But you can help me, if you want?'

Addie smiled. Jude was back. He was so proud of that watering can.

She supported one end of the can while Jude tilted it above the primroses; drizzled the water around the base of each of the plants, as Sam had shown him.

'I'm seeing Mam next week,' Addie said. 'Well, I might be,' she corrected, worried that this might upset Jude all over again. Tim hadn't said anything about him seeing *his* mam.

But it wasn't a might. Mam would be there, for sure.

Jude looked up. Water splashed over Addie's shoes. She pretended not to notice.

'I'm supposed to meet her in a café,' Addie said. 'With Penny.'

'Is your mum better now?' Jude asked. He pushed hair from his forehead, his eyes wide; worried. 'Are you going home soon?'

'She's a bit better. But she's got to stay longer at that special place and learn more things.' Addie stood up and dried her hands. 'So she can do her painting and feel happy again.'

'*Sunni's* mum doesn't like learning things,' Jude said. He put down the watering can.

'The social workers was helping her learn how to be Sunni's mum, only it didn't work.' His brow crinkled. 'That's why Sunni gets grumpy.'

'She's just grumpy because I'm here,' Addie said. 'She hates sharing her room. She hates *me*.'

Jude shook his head. 'No, she doesn't, Addie,' he said,

his eyes wide with worry. 'It's not your fault. It's cos she's sad. About her –' He stopped, bit his lip. 'I'm not s'pposed to say about it . . .' He looked around, as if Sunni might be listening, about to jump out at any moment.

'It's OK, Jude,' Addie said. 'You don't have to tell me. Not if you promised.' She looked away. She wasn't interested in anything to do with Sunni anyway. She bent down, brushed her hand over a nearby cluster of primroses. 'Can I pick some of these?' she asked.

Jude opened and closed his mouth.

'Only a couple. Please. I want to copy them. For Mam. For a present.'

Jude sighed. He held up one hand, pinned down his little finger with his thumb. 'Three,' he said. 'Just three.'

The delicate stems were covered in tiny hairs and surprisingly strong. Addie had to tug hard to break them free. The petals were waxy on her fingers. She could see bits of sky through them if she held them up against the spring sun. 'Beautiful, Jude,' she said. 'They're so beautiful.'

Jude smiled his small, quick smile. He searched her face.

'You know like I've got Thomas?' he said. Addie nodded.

'Sunni's got a sister now. An' she's better than Sunni

cos her mum's keeping *her*. That's what Sunni says.'

'Oh.' Addie wondered if this was true. Sunni said lots of things. Made up lots of things.

Maybe she just wanted all the attention for herself.

Well, Sunni would be happy soon, anyway. Because Addie would be gone.

Mam was *nearly* better. She must be, if Penny was letting her come to the café. Addie would be home in no time.

The foal didn't want to go back in the barn. Jude had to lean against his bottom while Addie bribed him with a handful of fresh straw.

'He likes it best outside now,' Jude said.

'I know,' Addie said. 'He wants to get back to the moor to find his mam.'

Jude nodded. 'Don't want him to go,' he said. 'Do you?'

'No,' Addie said. 'But . . .' Something heavy settled on her chest. She stroked the foal's cheek, swallowed hard. 'But he wants to go home, don't you?' The foal blinked his long lashes; stared his deep, soft stare. 'He *needs* to go home.'

Addie took a deep breath in; decided. 'There's people coming to look at him next week,' she said. 'You know, to say if he's proper Exmoor pony and if he's allowed back on the moor.'

Jude nodded. 'What if he's not, though?'

'Then we've got to take him back there. You and me. Right?'

'Can we?' Jude said. '*How* can we?'

'Of course we can. We have to.'

'But if you go home, Addie . . .'

'Then you'll have to do it.'

Jude's eyes filled. He ran his hand over the foal's flank. The foal flicked his tail from side to side. Jude pulled his arm away.

'He won't let me,' he said. 'If you're not there.'

'If he doesn't go back, he'll get sold, Jude. Gabe said. And some rich kids will ride him and plait his mane and make him jump stupid fences.' Addie's nails dug into her palms. 'And he won't see his mam ever again. Or his brothers and sisters.'

Jude's face darkened; brightened again. 'Sunni can help me,' he said.

'No, Jude!' Addie grabbed his arm. 'You can't say anything to Sunni. She'll tell. She's kind to you but she

133

hates me. And don't tell Gabe either. He'll go all grown-up and worried and stop you. You've got to promise.'

Jude's eyes slid away from Addie's. He looked up at the roof of the barn, as if he might find something he needed among the dusty rafters and giant cobwebs.

'I can't do promises,' he said. He wiped the sleeve of his coat across his face. 'I promised Thomas. I said I'd look after him. But I couldn't. Not proper.' His voice was small, far away, like it might be about to get lost again. His chin trembled, sank on to his chest. He wrapped his arms round his body, as if to protect himself from something that Addie couldn't see.

The foal pushed his head towards Jude, nudged at his arms, nuzzled his cheek.

'You look after your primroses, Jude, don't you?' Addie said. 'You're the best at looking after those.' She watched Jude's shoulders shake. He was crying the quiet tears. The ones that hurt the most.

Should she put her arm round him? Would he let her? How did Ruth always know what to do to help him? Addie wished she was here.

She imagined baby Thomas crying in his cot. She thought of Jude, lifting him into his thin arms, giving him the last of the milk and singing him to sleep.

She wondered about their mam and dad, who kept leaving them all alone.

'It wasn't your fault, Jude,' she said. 'Mams and dads are supposed to look after babies.' She placed a hand on his shoulder. 'And boys who are only six.'

She stroked the foal's nose, ran her finger over the tiny patch of white hair on his forehead. 'Don't worry, Jude,' she said. 'We'll get this little one home before I go. We'll do it together.'

NINETEEN

Addie put her primroses in a jar on the kitchen table, next to the jug of bluebells Gabe had brought from the forest. Addie would draw those for Mam too. Blue was her favourite colour.

'Have them a bit closer, if you want, Addie,' Ruth said. 'So you can see better.' She pushed the flowers across the table. The bluebells nodded on their long stalks.

Jude leaned in towards them, sniffed; sneezed. 'Spicy,' he said.

'Sticky too,' Sunni said. She pulled a flower from the jug and trailed the stem over Addie's hand. Jude backed away.

'It's OK, Jude,' Sunni said, 'I won't put any on you. They're poisonous. That's why Gabe got in trouble for picking them.'

Jude got down from his chair and stood back from the table.

'Sunni . . .' Ruth said.

Addie stared at Sunni. 'Why d'you always make things up?' She swivelled round on her chair to look at Ruth. 'Ruth wouldn't keep them in the kitchen if they were poisonous, would you, Ruth?'

'No, love,' Ruth said. She tousled Sunni's hair and pulled a bloom from the jug to show Jude. 'It's true that the actual plants are poisonous. You wouldn't want to eat them. But the flowers are so lovely, aren't they? We used to collect armfuls of bluebell flowers when I was a little girl.' She trailed her fingers through the drooped blue heads. 'And so did lots of other people. That's the problem. And that's why Gabe should know better. Even if he was only trying to do something nice for his ma.' She slipped the bluebell back into the water. 'There aren't too many proper British bluebells left now. They're dying out, so we're not supposed to pick them any more.'

'Is it the law?' Jude said.

Sunni cupped her ear with one hand. 'Oooh,' she said. 'I think I can hear police sirens . . .'

'It *is* the law, Jude,' Ruth said. 'But don't worry. Sunni's only teasing you. The law is just to make sure that bluebells will always be around for people to look at in the future.'

'So they're endangered,' Addie said. 'Like the Exmoor ponies.'

'That's it,' Ruth said.

Sunni flopped down in the chair opposite Addie, fiddled with a coloured pencil. 'Like the *real* Exmoor ponies, anyway,' she said. 'Not half-bloods like Addie's precious baby.'

Addie felt heat rise in her face. Sunni wasn't just mean; she was stupid as well. 'The foal's not a half-*anything*,' she hissed. 'He's just himself. And he's perfect.'

'Sunni, let's wait and see what the pony experts say, shall we?' Ruth handed Jude his colouring book and pencils, gave Addie the watercolour pencils she had brought from home. Mam's watercolour pencils. In the box with her name on the top in black letters.

'And try to be nice to each other now, please. Maybe you'd like to sketch something too, Sunni? How about one of those beautiful birds you and Mira saw?'

'I was just *saying*.' Sunni folded her arms across her chest. 'Anyone can see that foal's not a pure-blood now his winter coat's nearly gone.' Her eyes darted across Addie's face and hair. 'He's not the right colour.'

'Sunni, come with me. Now. We need a bit of a chat,' Ruth said, her expression severe for the first time since

Addie had met her. 'And a bit of fresh air. Then you can have a think about what you need to say to Addie.' She held open the door.

Sunni shoved her chair back and flounced across the room. 'I wouldn't draw those bluebells if I were you, Addie,' she said from the doorway. 'They're evidence. Gabe might get arrested if anyone sees what you've done.'

Ruth ushered Sunni from the room. 'Back in a minute,' she said. 'Just shout if you need me, you two.'

Jude sidled up to Addie. 'Sunni's only joking,' he said. 'She's just being silly.'

Addie looked at him. Sunni was his friend. She'd given up her treehouse. For him and for Thomas. 'Course she is,' she said. 'She's hilarious.'

It would be no good relying on Jude to keep their plans for the foal a secret from Sunni. Not for long, anyway. Addie would need to be careful about what she told him. 'Come on, Jude,' she said. 'Let's see if we've got the right colours and get drawing.'

She sorted through Mam's box until she found the perfect blue and a light apple-green. She began to draw.

Jude leaned close to her, watched as the bell-like blooms and long green stems came to life on her paper pad. He pushed his packet of crayons in front of her. 'Do primroses now,' he said. 'My primroses. Please, Addie.'

Addie's hand hovered above the packet of coloured pencils. 'What, with these?' Nobody was allowed to use Jude's crayons. Nobody was even allowed to touch them.

Jude nodded. 'But don't press hard. 'Case they break.'

Addie sharpened a dark green crayon. She drew the wide, crinkled primrose leaves, pencilled in the dark veins, like Mam had showed her. She outlined petals in soft grey and filled them in with lemon yellow, pressing lightly on the paper to achieve their delicate shade.

Jude watched, chin in hands. 'Wow,' he said, every so often. 'Wow, Addie.'

Addie held her drawing up to the light. 'Finished,' she said. 'Now my mam will see your primroses too, Jude.'

Jude reached for the sketch and laid it on the table. He traced the edge of a flower with one finger. 'It's pretty,' he said. 'Like a real one.'

'You draw some now,' Addie said. 'For Thomas. Tim can tell the foster carers to put your picture over his cot, so he can see it every day.'

Jude clutched Addie's drawing to his chest. 'I can't do it right,' he said.

'You can,' Addie said. 'It *will* be right,' she said. 'For Thomas.' She handed him the green crayon.

Jude chewed at the end of it. 'You,' he said. 'You do it.'

Addie opened his sketch book. 'Here,' she said. 'Look. Draw them here, next to this one.' She pointed to a picture of Jude with the foal: the first picture he had drawn of himself with a smile. The first picture he had drawn of himself with a mouth at all. 'You can give Thomas that one as well. It's really special.'

Jude looked up at Addie. His eyes caught the light from the window.

'Will the magic work for Thomas too?' he said.

'What?'

Jude bent his head closer. 'The magic. From the foal. Will it make Thomas's legs better?'

'What do you mean, Jude?'

'You know. How the foal made me talk again.' He held his hand to his face and whispered behind it. 'Does magic work in a picture?'

Addie stared at him. The kitchen was silent except for the hum of the fridge. The wind outside suddenly stilled, as if listening for Addie's answer.

'It might, Jude,' she said. She slotted the green crayon into the sharpener, turned it. A thin shaving of wood curled on to the table. 'You never know.'

Jude swept shavings into his hand, put them in his

pocket. He lined up his crayons in front of him and began to draw. When Ruth and Sunni came back into the room, he bent low over the table, guarded his work with one arm curled round the page.

Sunni had Ruth's laptop under her arm. She slammed it down on the table next to Addie. 'You can have my turn with this, if you want,' she said.

'And?' Ruth said.

'Sorry.' Sunni's eyes slid sideways towards Ruth. 'For being mean.'

'Well done, Sunni.' Ruth handed her a bowl of fat green apples and a knife with rope twisted round the handle. 'Now, want to help me make this apple pie? You're the best apple peeler I know. But wash those hands first, mind; we don't want soil with our apples.' She smiled across at Addie.

'We've been planting veg, Addie,' she said. 'Lettuce, peas and beans.'

'In my own vegetable patch,' Sunni said. 'Just mine.' She went to the sink, turned on the tap. 'But you can have some of my vegetables, Jude, when they're ready.'

She shook water from her hands as she walked back to her seat. Small spatters appeared on Addie's drawing, blurring the message she had written for Mam, underneath the jar of bluebells. Addie would have to start again.

'We thought you could all have a patch of garden, actually,' Ruth said. 'You can all choose some seeds to plant and help them grow. Sunni grew some fantastic carrots last year, didn't you, love?'

Sunni grinned. 'Better than yours,' she said. 'And I'm going to beat you with my peas this time too.'

'I'm sure.' Ruth laughed. 'You have green fingers there.'

Jude looked across at Sunni, stared at her hands. 'Flowers,' he said. 'I want to grow flowers.'

Sunni twirled an apple in her hand, pointed the peeler at Addie. 'You did know vegetables come out of the ground?' she said. She dug the edge of her knife into the apple. A droplet of clear juice appeared and ran down the shiny green skin. 'Not just out of tins?'

'Very funny,' Addie said. She turned her chair away from Sunni and pulled her drawing pad on to her lap. She thought of her tiny garden at home: the grey gravel and dry, dusty, soil. Nothing grew there any more. Not even weeds. It might be nice to plant some seeds here on the farm; to see new shoots push through the dark earth, new leaves stretching towards the sun. To feel proud, like Jude with his meadow flowers.

But there'd be no time for that.

Addie would ask Ruth for some seeds that would grow indoors in a pot. Then she and Mam would watch them grow together.

Jude's primroses had flame-red leaves and orange flowers.

'Best primroses ever,' Addie said. 'Look, Ruth.'

'Lovely, Jude,' Ruth said. 'Sunshine flowers.'

Jude glanced at Addie's drawing again. 'It's rubbish,' he said. 'I did the colours wrong.' He scrunched his picture into a ball and shoved it into his pocket. Pencil shavings fell to the floor.

'No, that's brilliant, Jude. It's proper art.' Addie pulled the laptop towards her. 'Look, I'll show you.'

Sunni looked up from crimping the edge of Ruth's apple pie with a fork.

'In the snug,' Addie said. She scooped up the laptop and her drawings. 'Come on, Jude.'

Widget curled up beside Addie and Jude on the baggy sofa in the corner of the snug. Ruth brought milk and biscuits and settled herself in an armchair with some of her papers. Widget purred.

Addie showed Jude some of the things Mam had shown *her*: Van Gogh's giant, wavy sunflowers; Monet's lilies floating on blue-green rivers and ponds; Picasso's wild scribbles and sliding faces.

'See, Jude,' Addie said. 'You can draw things how you want; colour them how you want.'

Jude gazed at the images on the screen. Their colours danced in his eyes. 'Let's do more art,' he said. He jumped up and hurried from the room. The smell of baking apples and sweet pastry drifted in through the open door.

Ruth smiled. 'Well done, Addie,' she whispered.

Addie went back to the kitchen, sat at the table with Jude, listened to the excited scratch of his pencil and crayons, and smiled at him each time he looked up. But she didn't feel like doing any more drawing.

Art belonged to her and Mam. Had she given it away?

She put Mam's watercolour pencils back in their case and closed the zip. Tight.

TWENTY

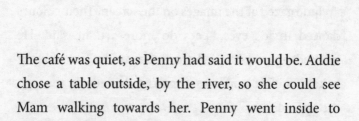

The café was quiet, as Penny had said it would be. Addie chose a table outside, by the river, so she could see Mam walking towards her. Penny went inside to order a milkshake that Addie knew she wouldn't be able to drink.

Addie took her bluebell picture from the back pocket of her jeans. She brushed the surface of the table with her hand, put the picture down and tried to smooth out the lines where it had been folded. She stood a silver salt cellar on top of it so that it wouldn't be blown on to the floor among the dust and crumbs.

A woman was feeding a baby at the next table, a shawl draped across her chest. The baby's small hand gripped one of her fingers. The woman smiled at Addie, then looked back down at her baby and stroked its cheek. The sky was almost-summer blue.

Addie chewed at her thumb. She looked up and down the riverside walkway, scanned the stone bridge and the paved path beyond. Which way would Mam come?

'Here we are, Addie,' Penny said, handing her the milkshake. 'I got you a strawberry one. And I thought we might need something to keep us all going.' She slid a plate of chocolate brownies in front of her. 'Your favourite, right?'

'What time is it?' Addie said. She couldn't even look at the chocolate brownies. She felt sick.

Penny took her phone from her bag. Sunlight flashed on its silver casing. 'Just a sec, Addie.' She scrolled at her phone with her thumb.

Addie stared out across the river. A duck dipped its head under the water, surfaced, swam back behind its babies and ushered them forward in a line through the dark green water.

'Ah,' Penny said. She put a hand on Addie's arm. 'Addie, there's a text from Lois – my colleague who was collecting your mum . . .'

Addie dragged her eyes to Penny's face. The sound of river water rushed in her ears.

'Your mum's not there, Addie. Lois has waited, but she's got to go in a minute, Addie. She's got another appointment.' Penny leaned closer, tucked a strand of Addie's wild hair behind her ear. Like Mam used to do. 'I'm sorry, sweetheart,' she said, 'but I don't think your mum's going to make it today.'

Addie batted Penny's hand away. 'She's coming,' she said. 'She wouldn't . . . She . . . she's coming by herself and she's just late. Mam's always late. For *everything*.' She stared into Penny's eyes; willed her to understand. 'She probably just got the time wrong. She gets muddled up. You know she does. I'm waiting till she gets here.' Addie crossed her arms, pressed her fingernails into her palms. 'You can go if you want.'

Penny smiled. The straight, sad smile: the one that said that she was right and Addie was wrong. 'Maybe this just isn't the right time, Addie,' she said. 'Maybe your mum's not ready after all.'

Addie's throat felt cold and tight. It ached, as if she'd eaten too much ice cream much too quickly. She covered her face with her hands; wished she could bury her head in the foal's warm neck and hear his heartbeat, strong and sure in her ears.

She pictured Mam walking across the bridge towards the café. Her red-gold hair lifted as she moved, spread around her face like sunshine; her blue velvet bag swung from one shoulder – the bag Addie had made for her birthday. Mam was smiling her old smile; holding out her arms to Addie. She smelled of paint and clay and apple shampoo.

Addie had dreamed it a hundred times.

She sat up straight, stared Penny in the eye. 'She's *coming*,' she said. She climbed up on her chair, scanned the street, the bridge, the riverbank. 'Which way is the bus station?'

'Addie, sit down, sweetheart. Please,' Penny said. 'Have your drink, then we'll go and find somewhere quieter to have a talk about things.' She slid Addie's milkshake across the table towards her.

Bubbles drifted across the top of the glass. Addie watched them burst against the side. She saw another glass: the tilt of dark wine inside it. She saw the wine disappear and slither, ruby red, across Mam's eyes. Saw it steal her away.

Today it was supposed to give her back.

Addie's head felt tighter and tighter inside, like it might burst, too.

'I'm waiting here,' she said. She threw herself back down in her chair and shoved the glass of milkshake towards Penny. It toppled and fell, rolled to the floor.

Penny jumped backwards, stood up and brushed at the spatters on her white shirt.

A slow pink river spread across the table; drip, drip, dripped from the edge on to the chair meant for Addie's mam.

Addie snatched the bluebell picture on to her lap. She looked down at the growing puddle of milk by her feet. Pieces of glass protruded from it: large and jagged; small and sharp. Treacherous islands in a pink sea.

A waitress hurried over with a dustpan and brush. 'Not to worry,' she said. 'I'll be back with a mop.' She bent to sweep up the glass.

Penny dabbed at the table with paper napkins. She said sorry to the waitress three times. She didn't say sorry to Addie.

Addie pointed at Penny. 'It was her fault,' she said to the waitress. 'Let her do it.'

A purple-haired girl on the next table stood up to leave. She grinned at Addie. 'Go, girl,' she mouthed, and lobbed a fat chip into the river. Two ducks slid under the water, emerged, spread their wings and reared up in challenge. She threw another.

A seagull sailed low above Addie's head, screeched, and landed on the nearby metal sign. It stared across at Addie with half-closed eyes, then swooped in and snatched a chunk of her untouched chocolate brownie with its hooked beak. Its great white wings beat the air as it took off with its prize. Crumbs skittered in the draught, landed in Addie's lap. The mother at the next table called to the waitress for her bill and drew the shawl closely round her sleeping baby.

'Ugh! Horrible, vicious things, seagulls,' Penny said, pulling the plate with the remains of the brownie quickly away from Addie. 'Nasty sharp beaks and claws.' She looked around, looked upwards; scanned the sky with one hand held over her eyes.

'He was just hungry, that's all,' Addie said. 'And he's gone now, anyway.'

Penny grabbed her purse from her bag and put two pound coins on the table for the waitress. 'Let's move over there.' She pointed to the riverbank. 'Come on, Addie. Quickly. We can sit on the grass and feed the rest of this cake to the ducks, instead of those greedy gulls. And you can still see the café while we talk. OK?'

They waited for an hour. People clattered over the bridge, wandered up and down the street, took seats in the café. Waitresses wiped tables. Penny threw cake for the ducks. They didn't seem to want it.

Addie held on tightly to her bluebell picture.

The sun faded. The surface of the river shivered.

Mothers and fathers pulled jackets from bags, tried to coax children into wearing them. Penny kept talking, explaining, wondering how Addie was doing. Addie heard her questions from the end of a long tunnel. She was floating there. It was lonely and cold.

Mam hadn't come.

Mam wasn't *going* to come.

'Addie? Addie, sweetheart!'

Fingers brushed Addie's cheek.

Penny. What was she saying? Addie tried to focus on her face. It was blurry at the edges.

'We really are going to have to make our way home now, Addie,' Penny said, 'so I'm not too late for my meeting. But then I'll go straight to Riverfields and see what I can find out about your mum. I promise. My guess is that she felt scared, when it came to it.' Penny leaned in closer. 'Your mum feels guilty, Addie. And that's because she loves you very much.' She sat back again, held out her hand, palm upwards. 'I think it's going to rain. Let's make our way home now, love.'

Addie blinked. Heat pulsed through her, dragged her back into the café with its empty tables, back into the empty day. She heard her own voice: loud. Angry.

'Home? It's not home. It's a stupid farm for kids with

stupid parents who don't want them any more. Well, my mam does want me. She just got sick, OK? So, if you'd all stop making her feel bad, and stop getting her all muddled up, she'll be better and we can go back to our proper home. Together.'

Addie scrambled to her feet. She turned and ran. Her legs felt strange, not quite under her control. She had no idea where she was going.

Penny's purple heels clattered along the pavement behind her. Seagulls wheeled and cried overhead.

The air was thick. Addie's chest ached. She thought of the foal waiting in the barn, listening for her footsteps. Calling for her. Wondering if *she* had left him, too.

She slowed down and let the now frantic Penny catch up with her.

When she climbed inside the car, Addie remembered that she'd left Mam's bluebell picture on the grass. By now, in this wind, it would be in the river, drifting with the ducks; dissolving into nothing among unwanted cake and slimy green weed.

Penny glanced at Addie every few seconds on the drive home, as if afraid that she might open the door and escape.

Addie wished she *could* escape. Escape from being Addie: Addie whose dad ran away – far away – back to the other side of the world where he was born; Addie whose mam ran away and got lost in her bottles; Addie, who made them both disappear.

She stared out through the windscreen. Dark clouds rolled across the sky, hung above the road ahead; washed the new colour from the moor.

Penny slowed the car as they approached a sharp bend in a wide sweep of road. Addie glimpsed the frightened eyes of a red stag, saw the flash of its white rump as it fled for cover.

Penny gave a small, excited shriek. 'How wonderful,' she said.

Addie ignored her. She hoped they hadn't scared the stag too badly.

Closer to the farm, sheep and young lambs stood clear of the trees; gathered in the centre of the meadows, waiting. Gabe's storm was coming, after all.

By the time Penny parked behind the Oaktree farmhouse, every bit of nearly-summer-blue sky was gone.

Addie didn't want to see Ruth. She didn't want Ruth's soft eyes pulling her tears from their hiding place in front of everyone; not in front of Sunni's smug, smiling face.

'I've got to look after my foal,' she told Penny. 'Tell Ruth she doesn't need to come and find me. I'm fine.' She slammed the car door shut and headed for the barn.

A few dry leaves blew across the courtyard. They scuttled like frantic insects around Addie's feet, swirled in the air; followed Addie in through the barn door.

The foal whinnied loudly. His eyes shone as he held Addie in his gentle gaze.

Addie threw her arms round his neck.

'She didn't come,' she said. 'She knew I was waiting for her, but she still didn't come.' She pressed her face into the foal's wiry mane, breathed in his earthy scent.

She cried for Mam, cried for herself, cried for the foal whose mother might be calling for him in the lonely forest.

Calling, still calling.

Waiting for him to come home.

Addie had no idea how long she lay curled with the foal on his bed of straw. But when she stirred, the light was soft in the barn and the foal's mane was wet beneath her cheeks.

'Thank you,' she said.

She got to her feet, took his face between her hands. 'Don't worry,' she said. 'You're going back to see *your* mam. It's time. I'm taking you back to her – and *no one* is going to stop me.'

TWENTY-ONE

Addie lay in bed, listening as the farmhouse settled into another night. Outside the window, everything was still.

The storm had not arrived. Sam had said it might blow over. But the air felt thick and heavy with waiting, as if the world was fearful of what was to come.

Addie's chest was heavy too. Like when Darren Oates shoved her over in the playground. He'd stood laughing with his friends as she scrabbled to her feet, winded and desperate not to cry. Addie remembered the sharp sting of gravel in her skin. She tried to feel it again now, to blot out the ache in her stomach, the questions in her head.

Penny had kept her promise and put Mam on the line. But Mam couldn't explain why she had broken hers. Her voice had been too quiet, as if that was broken too.

If she let her eyes close, Addie saw the bridge by the river: saw it sway in the wind as if it might break free and float away on the water. She saw the seagull with its cruel beak, heard its plaintive scream as it wheeled away and disappeared among the clouds. She saw Mam's empty chair at the café table, with its gathering pink puddle and splinters of translucent glass.

Addie pushed the picture away. She thought of the foal on his bed of straw, tried to conjure his warm presence beside her in her bed.

How would she manage on the farm without him?

But her mind was made up. Penny might be able to keep *her* away from her mam, but no one was going to keep the foal away from his. Addie would make sure of it.

She needed to do something quickly, before Sam's 'experts' stuck their noses in. Or he might be taken from the farm, sold to strangers and never get to go home.

Never get to see his mam. Not ever, ever again.

Addie strained to hear above a sudden whip of wind at the bedroom window. Everything inside the house was quiet. Sunni's shadowed shape was motionless under her covers.

Addie slid to the floor. She slipped past Sunni's bed and crept along the landing to Jude's room, careful to avoid any creaky boards.

Jude's curtains were open. He was sitting at the end of his bed, a small statue in the bright moonlight that spilled across the room. Had he sensed that she would come tonight?

Addie held a finger to her lips. She closed the door and sat down beside him.

'We've got to do it,' she whispered. 'We've got to get the foal home. Quickly.'

'Now?' Jude glanced at the window, looked back at Addie, his eyes wide; afraid.

'Tomorrow. Night.'

'Why?'

'Those pony people are coming the next day. Sam said. They might take him away.'

'It'll be dark.'

'Yes. Easiest to sneak away then, while everyone's sleeping. But we've got to make a proper plan.'

Jude chewed at his bottom lip, pulled the sleeves of his pyjama jacket down over his hands. 'The foal's only a baby,' he said. 'He'll be scared of the dark.'

'He'll be fine,' Addie said. 'And so will you. You're the bravest boy I know.' She smiled at him. 'Anyway, there's going to be a full moon tomorrow. Gabe said.'

Jude looked down. His lashes threw long shadows

159

on his cheeks. 'We'll be sad, though,' he said. 'When the foal goes home.'

Addie nodded. The ache in her stomach pushed its way into her throat. She swallowed hard. 'But the foal will be happy. We'll be glad if he's happy, won't we?'

Jude's hands twisted in his lap. 'Your mum said she's taking you home too, didn't she? When you saw her?' He drew a shuddering breath. 'I won't be brave when *you* go.'

Addie got up, crossed to the window and peered outside. Widget was stalking across the yard below. He stopped, hunched down low. He lifted his head and looked up towards Addie, as if suddenly aware that she was watching him. His eyes glowed red in the moonlight.

'You are, aren't you?' Jude stood behind her. One hand hovered above Addie's shoulder, like a pale moth afraid to land. 'Going home?'

Addie watched her reflection in the windowpane, saw her lips form words that had pressed at the inside of her head since that afternoon by the river.

'No,' she said. 'I'm not going home.'

The moth hand touched down, lifted again.

'Not ever?' Jude said.

Addie closed her eyes, blotted out the ghost girl in

the window: the girl whose mam didn't love her as much as the bottles in her bag.

'Just, not yet,' she said. She hoped that bit was true. Her eyes burned.

'Isn't your mam all better then?' Jude said. 'What did she say?'

Addie turned to face him. 'We're supposed to be making a plan,' she said. 'Get your pencils and paper out.'

She heard something.

There it was again. A soft shuffling – outside the door.

Who was there?

Addie held her finger to her lips. 'Quiet, Jude,' she whispered.

The door clicked open.

Sunni. Her dark glass hair, the swing of her red dressing gown in the doorway. How long had she been out there? How much had she heard?

She stepped into the room. 'What are you two up to then?'

'None of your business,' Addie said. 'Go back to bed.'

Sunni eased the door shut, pressed her back against it. 'Well, it *is* my business because you woke me up in the middle of the night.' She slid her bracelets up her arm, watched them clatter back together at her wrist.

'And anyway,' she said, her chin in the air, 'I already know. You weren't exactly whispering.'

'You can't tell,' Jude said.

'Shut up, Jude,' Addie said. She glared at Sunni, crossed the room and eased the door closed.

'If you must know,' Addie said, 'Jude had one of his dreams.' She looked over at him; stared hard into his wide eyes. 'And he was telling me things about it – private things, weren't you, Jude?'

Jude nodded. His eyes darted from side to side.

Sunni threw herself on to Jude's bed. 'You're useless at lying, Jude,' she said. 'And I thought you were my friend. Why are you taking *her* side?'

'I am your friend,' Jude said. He put his hands on his hips. 'But I'm *Addie's* friend too. Don't be mean to her. She's really sad.'

'Jude! *Shut* up,' Addie said.

Sunni tipped her head on one side, pulled a strand of hair through her lips.

'What happened then?' she said, as if Addie wasn't even in the room. 'Last I heard, she was off back to Wonder-Mam.'

'Tell her, Addie,' Jude said.

'Yes, tell me, Addie,' Sunni said. 'Or I'll tell Ruth

you're making another one of your crazy plans and she'll tell your social worker.' She crossed her arms. 'Then see what happens . . .'

Jude stood tall, folded his arms across his chest.

'No, Sunni, don't. Cos if you do, I'll tell about *your* secret . . .'

Sunni sprang to her feet. She grabbed Jude's arms. 'You dare! You promised!'

Jude froze.

'Leave him, Sunni,' Addie said. 'He doesn't like it.'

Sunni slumped back down on the bed. 'Sorry, Jude,' she said.

Jude positioned himself between Addie and Sunni 'You two got to make friends,' he announced. He sat down next to Sunni. 'Because you both got sad things. And you both got 'portant secrets.' He nodded, as if he had no doubt at all that he was right.

Addie heard Ruth's softness in his words. A smile tugged at the corners of her mouth, then it was gone. She held up her hand. 'Shush. Listen,' she whispered.

The floorboards creaked. The landing light clicked on. Yellow light shone under Jude's door.

Ruth appeared, rubbing at her eyes.

'Jude had a bad dream,' Sunni said. 'Didn't you, Jude?'

Jude nodded. 'Awful-terrible.'

'Oh dear, Jude,' Ruth said. 'How about I read you a story then, sweetheart? You choose a book.' She pulled back Jude's covers and plumped his pillows.

She smiled at Addie and Sunni – the same smile she gave Gabe when he said he hadn't eaten the last of the chocolate fingers. 'Thank you, girls,' she said. 'But off you go now. Back to bed. Sam says you're both helping with the new lambs in the morning – bright and early. So you'd better get some sleep.' She yawned. 'Addie, let me know if you can't settle, OK?' She smiled her warm smile and opened the book that Jude had given her.

Jude lay back against his pillows and pulled his duvet up under his chin. 'I need *two* stories, Ruth,' he said. 'My dream was special scary this time.'

'Ruth didn't believe us, you know,' Sunni said. 'About Jude's dream. She always knows when people aren't telling the truth. She always knows everything. That's why you need my help . . .'

'No thanks,' Addie said. She sat up, flicked on her

164

bedside lamp. 'I wouldn't tell *you* anything. And anyway, there isn't any plan, OK?'

'Suit yourself,' Sunni said. 'I know all about it, anyway, like I said.'

'Well, you don't,' Addie said. 'Because there's nothing to know.'

She switched off the light and stared into the darkness. What exactly had Sunni heard? Perhaps it was just bits and pieces. Maybe she thought Addie was planning another attempt at getting home. Well, good – if she did – because Sunni wouldn't spill the beans on *that* plan. She'd be more than happy to see Addie run away – and stay away.

So would Addie. But until Mam was home, there was nowhere for her to run *to*.

No *one*.

Her chest tightened. She swallowed hard. She couldn't think about Mam just now. She had to focus on the foal: make her plan.

'Just so you know,' Sunni said, 'there's no way you're taking Jude on one of your stupid escape missions.' She yawned. '*He's* much too nice to be supper for the Beast of Exmoor.'

Addie sighed, pulled her duvet over her head.

'And in case you're wondering,' Sunni said, 'the Beast of Exmoor is a giant cat that stalks the moor looking for food. Especially at lambing time. Which is when *people* go missing too.'

Addie heard the clink of bracelets, the creak of bedsprings. Sunni's voice became a whisper. 'And no one *ever* finds them . . .'

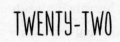

TWENTY-TWO

Jude didn't want his breakfast the next morning. His cheeks were scarlet.

Ruth laid a hand on his forehead. 'Hot,' she said. 'Burning. Back to bed for you, young man.' She took Jude by the hand. 'Let's get you tucked up with a nice cold drink.'

'I'll need to stay in with Jude today,' Ruth said. 'I'll not be able to help out with the lambing now.' She glanced at the kitchen clock. 'Gabe, can you pop over and tell your dad for me, love? If there's still a lot happening, he might want to ring over to Jackson's farm and see if one of their lads can help. He's been out there for hours. He'll be exhausted.'

'I'll tell him,' Sunni said. She dabbed at the corners of her mouth with her napkin, pushed back her chair. 'But he won't need extra help. He's got Gabe and me. And Addie, I *suppose*,' she added, 'if she's not too busy.' She stared meaningfully at Addie.

Addie ignored her. She'd already promised to help Sam and had fed the foal extra early so that she could. Helping out would make the day pass quickly; calm her nerves about the night-time adventure to come. And it might stop Sunni being too suspicious. She couldn't risk her saying something to Ruth.

But Addie felt more anxious than ever now that Jude was sick. Was she brave enough to do this all by herself?

It was lucky that Ruth and Sam were going to be so busy. Otherwise, they'd notice that Addie seemed jittery and preoccupied. They'd ask questions. Because Sunni was right: Ruth had this way of 'knowing things' about you. And as for Sam, he didn't miss a thing.

'OK, Sunni,' Ruth said, gathering a wilting Jude closer to her, 'thank you.' She pointed to a tartan flask by the kettle. 'Take him that, would you, love? He'll be needing a hot drink.'

Sunni grabbed the flask and was gone.

'Get yourself over to the shed as quickly as you can, Gabe,' Ruth said. 'Your dad must be exhausted. There were some tricky births overnight and a problem with a couple of the new mums.'

Gabe looked up from his breakfast – his second that morning – an enormous plate of bacon and eggs. 'Don't worry, Ma,' he said. He waved his fork at Addie, took a bite of toast. 'Cavalry's on its way.'

Addie swallowed a mouthful of porridge, pushed her bowl away. She wasn't hungry.

'Oh, and Addie,' Ruth called from the doorway, 'no need to take the foal to the meadow this morning; he can have a run this afternoon, when the pony folk are here. They'll want to get a look at him on the move before they decide anything, I expect.'

'Today?' Addie said, trying to hide her panic. 'Sam said they were coming tomorrow.'

'He'll have got his days confused, Addie. We've been so busy with the lambing and everything.' Ruth tilted her head on one side. A long strand of hair slipped free from her untidy bun and hung across her face. 'I know the foal's your special friend, sweetheart. Let's just see what they say today, OK?'

Jude leaned against her; his face redder than ever. 'The foal doesn't like them,' he said, his voice cracked and dry. 'He only likes us.'

Ruth stroked his head. She smiled at Addie. 'That foal's not going anywhere yet. Not today, whatever happens. Sam said to tell you that's a promise. OK?'

Addie listened to her quick steps on the stairs, the

soothing murmur of her voice when Jude began to cough.

Ruth and Sam were being kind in trying to understand about the foal. But they didn't.

Addie felt heavy inside.

It was no use pretending. Sunni was right. Now that the foal was growing up, he wasn't like the Exmoor ponies Addie had seen on moorland drives with Sam and Ruth. He didn't resemble the foals in the pictures she'd found on the internet. He had the same dark mane and tail. The same pale muzzle and forelegs. But while those Exmoor ponies all had dark brown or red coats, his was paler, more grey than brown. Beneath his flanks, he was mottled like the wings of the doves nesting in the rafters of the barn.

And then there was the new mark on his forehead: white and feathered; a small snowflake between his almond eyes.

White marks were against the rules.

Addie already knew what the pony people would say.

Her foal wasn't a pure-blood. He wouldn't be allowed to go home.

There was no time to waste.

Tonight might be Addie's only chance to make sure that he did.

She would not let him down.

She scraped the remains of her porridge into the bin and dropped her bowl and spoon into the sink. She would go and help Sam, but she'd work on her plan to get the foal back to his mam at the same time.

A new plan. One that meant finding her way across the night-time moor all alone.

'Have you ever seen this Big Cat thing that's supposed to be on the moor?' Addie asked Gabe, as they pulled on their boots in the hallway.

Gabe grinned. 'Sunni, right?' he said. 'Been trying to spook you, has she?'

Addie shrugged. 'I know it's not real.'

'Some people think it is,' Gabe said. He zipped up his waterproof jacket, took a blue beanie hat from his pocket. He grinned at Addie. 'It's just an old folk tale, Addie. The only wild beast round here is Ma – when you drink milk straight from the carton, or scoff all the cheese. Now that *is* scary!'

He whistled for Flo. She appeared, as if by magic, eyes bright and keen.

Addie stroked her silky head. 'I'm not scared. I told you.'

She wasn't. The only thing that scared her was being away from Mam. And the papers in Penny's bag, with their black spider signatures and their lies. And anyway, Addie was going to get the foal safely home to *his* mam, whatever might be lurking in the darkness of the moor.

She took down her new coat from the peg.

'Put your old one on, I would, Addie,' Gabe said. 'It gets a bit messy in the lambing shed.'

Addie's old coat felt tight. It smelled different now: of wood smoke and baking. Addie pushed her fingers through the hole in the right-hand pocket and remembered other smells: the dusty hallway at home, the vinegar sting of the kitchen bin with its empty bottles and chip papers streaked with grease. The twisted tubes of paint that had lost their lids.

She opened the front door and took in a deep breath of clean, spring air; pushed the old smells away. When she *did* go home, there would be new smells, new tubes of paint. And the old Mam. The first one. The Mam that took Addie to the park on dark winter afternoons and pushed her on the scratched blue swings – higher and higher, to see if she could touch the moon. She never could. But it never mattered.

Flo hurried on ahead of Addie and Gabe, her ears pricked high. As they drew close to the lambing shed, Addie heard the thin bleat of lambs and a deeper note: a low, rumbling moan that was almost human.

'What's that noise?' she asked Gabe.

'One of the ewes,' Gabe said. 'About to give birth by the sound of it.'

He scooped up a bucket and placed it underneath a tap on the shed wall. Silvery water gushed into the bucket. Flo snatched at the flow of water. Her jaws snapped together as she tried to catch stray droplets in mid-air.

'Her favourite game,' Gabe said. 'She'd do that all day if I let her. Daft dog.' He turned off the tap. 'Game over, Flo,' he said. He looped the handle of the bucket over his arm and told Flo to wait. She lay down, her wet nose on her white paws.

Gabe pulled open the shed door. 'C'mon, Addie,' he said, above the sound of the lambs. 'Quick. You're about to see your first lambing.'

The lambing shed was much bigger than the foal's barn: more modern, with long, bright electric lights stretched across the ceiling. Sheep stood inside straw-lined pens, chewing slowly, while lambs fed from them on quivering legs. Other sheep lay alone, their bellies round and swollen.

Sam was kneeling in the pen nearest the door. A sheep lay on its side in front of him. It lifted its head and stared at Addie and Gabe as they came close. Its eyes bulged, white and wild.

'Hi, you two,' Sam said. He didn't look up. He ran his hand over the sheep's woolly flank. Almost there, girl,' he said.

'Brought you a sandwich.' Gabe pulled a foil-wrapped package from his pocket, put it down on the straw within Sam's reach.

'Very welcome,' Sam said. 'Soon as the little one's joined us, I'll enjoy that.'

The sheep called: a low, mournful sound, as if she was asking for help.

'Is her lamb coming right now?' Addie said.

'Reckon so,' Sam said. 'Want to watch?'

Addie nodded. She'd never seen anything being born before.

The sheep's abdomen lifted and fell in great waves. Her breath became loud and ragged.

'Is she all right?' Addie asked.

'She's fine,' Sam said. 'Doing great.' He eased a silvery wet bundle from the sheep's body, rubbed away red streaks of blood with handfuls of straw. A pink mouth opened in a small black face. Sam cleared it with one finger, held the lamb upside down; swung it from side to side by its long black legs. Round eyes opened and blinked in surprise.

Addie glanced up at Gabe. 'Why's Sam doing that?' she asked. 'It's cruel.'

Gabe shook his head. 'It's to clear the lamb's airways; make sure it can breathe OK. It's fine. Watch.'

The lamb bleated. Sam laid it down beside its mother's head. The ewe sniffed her baby's thin body, licked its mouth, nudged and nuzzled it into life.

Addie looked up at Sam. 'She loves it already, doesn't she?' she said.

'Aye.' Sam nodded. 'She's a natural mum, this one. Always the same. Motherhood comes easy to her.'

Addie watched as the newborn lamb tried to stand, pushing up on spindly hind legs, as the foal had done when he was first at the farm. The ewe got to her feet too, tired as she was. She stood patiently as her baby wobbled closer and rooted under her abdomen for milk.

How had the lamb felt being pulled from its mam's

warm belly into the bright, cold shed? Addie wondered.

Had the little creature been afraid?

She closed her eyes for a moment. She tried to imagine how it must have felt when she was growing inside Mam: safe and warm in the dim, muffled space where she was part of Mam and no one could see her. Or take her away.

She couldn't make the pictures come.

Sam sat back on his heels, wiped his hands with a bunch of straw. He took the lid off his flask. He poured steaming coffee, drained the cup in one gulp and stood up. He stretched his back straight; yawned.

'One more job,' he said. 'Stay there, you two. Gabe, check the old girl over, will you? See if she'll take a bit of feed. She's had a long night of it.' He scooped up the newborn lamb and walked to the other end of the shed. Addie heard Sunni's voice among the frantic cries of the lamb and the clatter of Sam's boots on the stone floor.

The new mother would not eat. She got to her feet, calling.

'She wants her baby,' Addie said. 'Why has Sam taken it? She's really worried.'

'You'll see,' Gabe said. 'In a minute.'

Sam walked towards them again a few moments

later. He was cradling two lambs now, each complaining in a voice which seemed too big for its tiny frame. He climbed back into the pen, held the lambs close together for a moment, then lowered them on to the straw. He ran his hands several times over each of them in turn and moved away. The mother sheep was quiet now.

Addie stared at Sam, then at Gabe. Did both lambs belong to this mother?

'Keep watching, Addie,' Sam said.

The sheep nudged at each lamb in turn. The lambs struggled to their feet, wobbling on their new legs. Their black noses disappeared into the sheep's wool. They began to feed from her in jerky movements, their short tails quivering as they drank. The ewe stood patient and still as the lambs fed, her eyelids half closed.

'Fantastic,' Gabe said. 'Job done.'

Sam smiled and nodded. 'Nice to see,' he said. He poured more coffee, turned to Addie. 'That second lamb's one of our "orphans", Addie. But I've transferred the scent of her own lamb, so the other little guy smells just like her own baby. She'll mother that one as well.'

'One orphan sorted, two to go,' Gabe said. Sunni's giving the others a bottle. I expect she'd like a hand, Addie.'

Addie was sure that was the last thing Sunni would want.

'But where are their mothers?' she said. 'Are they sick? Did they die?'

Gabe rubbed at his chin. Addie heard the rasp of his fingers on his dark stubble.

'One of the ewes died, yes, Addie. Her lamb was big. It got stuck when it was being born. The vet was here, but neither of us could do anything. It happens that way every now and again, love. Not often, thank goodness.' He smiled at Addie.

'What about the others?' Addie said.

'One of them's been ill. She's not strong enough to care for her youngster this time. Needs looking after herself. The other, well, she's just didn't take to being a mum.'

Addie stretched her neck, tried to see the other motherless lambs at the back of the barn. 'Will the others get new mams as well?' she said.

'Hope so, Addie,' Gabe said. 'Otherwise you might have to take over – you've done such a good job looking after that foal.' He grinned. 'We could move your bed in here for a bit.'

'I wouldn't mind,' Addie said. It would be better than sharing with Sunni.

'Proper little farmer in the making,' Sam said. 'Your mam will be very proud of you.'

He leaned over, washed his hands in a bucket of water.

Addie kicked at the straw under her feet. Would Mam be proud of her? Could she be, ever again?

TWENTY-THREE

Addie attached the leading rein to the foal's harness and led him from the barn. She didn't want to take him to see the pony people, but she had promised Ruth that she would. Sam was still busy in the lambing shed. Gabe was mucking out the pigs. Ruth was trying to settle Jude, who now had red spots on his stomach and arms which he was trying to scrub away.

'Chickenpox,' Ruth said. Addie felt sorry for Jude. She remembered chickenpox: the endless hot itch; the cold, sticky lotion that soothed it. Jude would hate it, poor thing. But if only he had waited until after the foal was home before getting ill.

The foal knew that something was different. He stood in the middle of the yard, snorted and refused to move – even when Addie coaxed him with a mint.

'It's OK,' Addie said. 'Someone just wants to look at you for a minute.' She smoothed his nose. 'Then, tonight,' she whispered in his ear, 'you're going to go back to your mam.'

The foal stepped backwards towards the barn. He tossed his head from side to side, his eyes wide, fearful.

Gabe appeared, blue dungarees rolled above dirty Wellington boots, a swill bucket over his arm. He raised a gloved hand at Addie. 'Little guy playing up, is he?' he asked.

'Don't think he's feeling well,' Addie said. 'Those people will have to come another day. Tell Sam.'

'Nice try, Addie,' Gabe said.

A mud-splattered jeep swung into the yard. The foal threw his head back, showed his strong white teeth and tried to rear up on his hind legs.

'Whoa, calm down, fella.' Gabe spoke in soothing tones. 'Careful, Addie,' he said. 'Wouldn't want to see you get clobbered. Never an attractive look, hoof prints on the face.'

'He wouldn't hurt me,' Addie said. She pointed towards the jeep. 'It's the jeep that he doesn't like. And the people inside it.'

A tall woman in jodhpurs and a yellow fleece jacket emerged from the driver's door. She raised a hand at

181

Addie and Gabe, before reaching into the back of the vehicle.

The foal shook his head and pulled away.

Gabe put a hand on Addie's arm. 'He's upset because you are, Addie. He knows you're anxious, so he is as well.' He looked into her face. 'Best let me, eh?'

Addie looked at the foal. He stared back at her. The whites of his eyes glinted; his left hoof scraped at the ground. Gabe was right. The foal always knew what she was feeling. He was the only one who did.

'You won't let them take him, will you?' she said.

'Nothing's going to happen today, Addie.' Gabe rested a gloved hand on her arm. 'Dad always keeps his promises.'

The woman was striding towards them now. A bald man jumped out of the jeep and caught up with her.

He was carrying a briefcase. There would be papers in there. Papers for deciding things.

Addie looked away.

She handed Gabe the rein. 'You've got to tell me what they say, OK? About the blood tests. If the foal's got to be sold, or whatever. If he's allowed to go home. Tell me *straight away*, OK?'

'Dad will, Addie,' Gabe said softly. 'He'll want to explain it all himself.'

Addie leaned in close to the foal, felt the twitch of his ear against her forehead. 'Don't you worry,' she whispered, 'it doesn't really matter what those people say. I'm not letting them take you anywhere. *I* promise, too.'

Addie knelt up on the kitchen window seat, craned her neck to find out what was happening with the foal. Was he calmer now? She couldn't see.

Two blackbirds landed in the yard. They pecked at the ground with their orange beaks, searching for insects that crept between the cobbles. Addie thought of their helpless babies, waiting wide-mouthed, high up in the oak trees around the farm.

She hoped the foal didn't think she had abandoned him.

She hoped Gabe was right about Sam's promises.

She hoped Mam would start keeping hers.

Sam kicked off his boots and rolled up his sleeves. He scrubbed at his nails in the square kitchen sink, wiped at spatters of muddy water on the white enamel.

'The foal's back in the barn, having a snooze,' he said. 'He behaved himself in the end.' He smiled at Addie, dried his hands on a faded red towel.

Addie noticed the blue veins that criss-crossed his arms like intersecting rivers on a map. 'What did they say?' she asked. 'The pony people?'

Sam filled the kettle and put it on the hob to boil. He took two striped mugs down from the cupboard. 'Tea?' he said. 'Or something else?'

Addie shook her head. 'Nothing. Thank you.' She studied Sam's face for answers.

He sat down in the rocking chair, scooted it closer to Addie. He rubbed his eyes and stifled a yawn. 'Sorry, love,' he said. 'I'm needing my bed.' He leaned forward, elbows on his knees. 'He's a beautiful young foal, Addie. You've done a great job there. Tony and Margaret were impressed with the both of you.' He smiled. 'And so am I.' His smile fell away. 'But he's not an Exmoor, Addie. Not a pure-bred.'

The kettle let out a piercing whistle. Sam got to his feet and lifted it from the hob. 'They only had to look at him, Addie,' he said. 'No surprise there.' He took milk from the fridge, poured some into his mug, sat down again. 'But the little guy's still a bit of a mystery. The blood results weren't entirely clear. But based on his coat, Tony thinks one of his parents could be a stray Dartmoor pony. Or maybe a mixed-breed that got into one of the herds somehow.'

Tony. Addie pictured the bald man with his briefcase full of tests, rules and decisions. She didn't like him. Or his briefcase. 'So our foal doesn't belong to either of them, then? They can't say what happens to him? Margaret? Or that Tony?'

Addie's heart quickened.

'Well, actually, there *is* another plan for him . . .' Sam drained his cup. 'Margaret's daughter runs an animal sanctuary. Not too far from here really. She's building a herd of wild ponies and she's keen to have him.' Sam put his empty mug on the floor beside his chair and looked Addie in the eye. 'It could be great for him, Addie. He'd be with other ponies; there'd be lots of space for him: plenty of fresh air and freedom. There'd be equine vets and proper pony folk to take care of him.'

'No. No way,' Addie said. She folded her arms across her chest. 'That's not happening.'

Sam rubbed his eyes and settled back in the rocking chair. 'I know you love that foal, Addie,' he said, his voice flat; tired. 'And I know why want him to go home, back to the moor. But Margaret and Tony say he wouldn't do well in the wild now, even if he *was* allowed back. He's been brought up here. He might not know how to survive out there; might not even be accepted into the herd. He lifted his arms, let them fall to his knees. 'I'm just a sheep and cow man, Addie. I've got to be guided by the experts. They know what they're talking about.'

'They *think* they know things –' Addie forced her words through her teeth – 'but they don't.' How could going to that sanctuary be good for him? A place miles away from all the sights and sounds and smells that he knew. Miles away from his herd. Miles away from his mam.

'You said he could be a riding pony for someone,' Addie said. Not that she was going to let that happen, either. But she had to play along. 'Somewhere *really* near here, near his home.' She sat forward on the edge of the window seat. 'Or he could just stay here, *couldn't* he? Why can't he?'

Sam shook his head. 'Wild ponies are herd animals, Addie. It might not be fair to keep him all alone. Not once he's older, anyway.'

'Fair?' she shouted. 'Stopping him from going back to his proper home is the thing that's not fair. No one cares about that, though, do they?'

Sam leaned towards Addie. 'That little foal was all alone when we found him, Addie,' he said, his voice quiet, gentle. 'Remember?' He cleared his throat. 'There was no sign of his mother.'

He looked into Addie's eyes. She had to look away. She watched Widget uncurl himself by the stove. He stretched out one of his hind legs and licked at it with his pink tongue.

'I think what matters now, Addie,' Sam said, 'is making sure that the foal goes somewhere he can settle properly, don't you?' He moved to sit on the window seat in front of Addie. 'Somewhere where he'll be safe and well looked after as he grows up. Where he can have a happy life and still do the things wild ponies need to do.'

Addie wanted to say that the foal would have all that back on the moor. With his mam. But she didn't trust herself to say anything more. She sometimes had the sense that Sam could see right inside her head, right into the middle of her.

'When?' she said. 'When will the sanctuary woman have to take him?'

'She can hold the sanctuary place for a fortnight. But she'd rather take him in the next day or two.' Sam painted a bright smile on his face. It didn't fit properly.

Addie knew that he was sorry to make her sad.

'Once the lambing's done,' Sam said, 'I can drive you and Jude over for a visit. How would that be?'

His face blurred; swam against the window glass. Addie wiped her eyes.

'What's the name of the sanctuary place?' she said. 'Can I borrow the laptop and look it up?'

Sam nodded. 'Of course, sweetheart.' He pinched the bridge of his nose, closed his eyes for a moment. 'Bring it in here, though, OK? You can show me what you find.'

Addie fetched the laptop from the snug. No one else was about. Gabe had taken Sunni off with Flo for more of her precious shepherding practice. Ruth was working upstairs, to keep Jude company. His dry cough and thin wails drifted down as Addie passed the foot of the stairs. She would go and see how he was later. And tell him the news. He would be worrying.

When she went back into the kitchen, Sam had nodded off in his chair. His head hung forward on to his chest. Addie thought of his long night in the lambing shed; his patient kindness towards the anxious ewes and their tiny lambs. His kindness to her. She felt a stab of guilt. Her plans for tonight would terrify him, even anger him, perhaps.

But Addie wouldn't think about that now. The foal needed her.

She opened the laptop, looked back at Sam. The rise and fall of his chest was slow and steady. While he dozed, unaware, she'd look up Winsford Hill and Withypool Common, where the nearest Exmoor herds could be found. She'd try to find directions from the farm. She could draw herself a map for later. And if she had the chance before Sam woke, she'd sneak some supplies from the kitchen for her night-time trip and hide them away.

She took a deep breath, pushed out the quiver of unease in her chest.

Who knew when Margaret's daughter might turn up to take the foal away? Sam had said she'd wait a bit. But Addie knew what happened when 'experts' had decided what was best. They made it happen.

Now, even more than ever, Addie needed to act tonight.

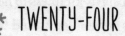

TWENTY-FOUR

Jude was allowed downstairs to watch television while Ruth made dinner. He lay on the sofa in the snug, wrapped in a blanket. His pale face was strewn with red spots; his huge eyes smaller and pink round the edges. He wriggled and scratched, but told Addie he was feeling much better now – he really was. Addie felt his determination in the air; his silent insistence that he should still be part of things.

How much should she say about her plans for later? She didn't want to leave him out. But he was tired and sick, more anxious than ever. He might give her away.

'Everything's sorted, Jude,' she said. 'For later. And don't worry. I'll be OK on my own –'

Sunni burst into the room, full of stories of her amazing dog-handling skills. Her excited voice rose above the hum of cartoon voices and crazy tunes. There was no chance to say any more to Jude.

Jude brushed the back of his hand across his eyes

and stared past Addie at the flickering images on the television screen. His shoulders sank.

Addie felt heavy and small.

Why did she always make people sad when she didn't mean to?

Ruth brought Jude some soup and ice cream. She sent Addie to have her dinner in the kitchen with the others, while she ate hers from a tray with Jude.

Addie was too nervous to be hungry, but she ate two helpings of beef stew. She needed energy for what lay ahead. Her stomach felt tight as she helped Gabe clear away the dishes and stack the dishwasher.

As Addie headed back to the snug, Sam came into the hall with Jude in his arms. Jude's damp head lolled against Sam's shoulder. His thin feet protruded from his blanket. There was an angry red spot on one of his white toes.

'Pretty much fell asleep in his ice cream,' Sam whispered. 'Poor little chap. But that's him for the night hopefully. A good sleep will work wonders.' He headed for the stairs.

Addie peered inside the snug. It was empty now. The television was still on. Pink elephants danced across the screen in frilled skirts, their trunks intertwined.

Addie pulled the plug from the wall. The smiling elephants disappeared.

Jude wouldn't be coming with her. When he woke in the morning, the foal would be gone. Just like Thomas.

Jude wouldn't have a chance to say goodbye this time either.

She hoped he would understand.

Addie told Ruth that she wanted an early night. She dragged her bag of supplies from underneath her bed and checked the contents: a map, a bottle of water, a hunk of bread, cheese, apples and four of Ruth's chocolate cookies wrapped in foil. So far, Ruth hadn't noticed that anything was missing. She was probably exhausted after her difficult day with Jude.

Addie bundled everything back inside her bag, along with her warmest jumper and Mam's lucky shell. She pushed the bag under her duvet, wriggled it down to the bottom of the bed. She would collect Sam's torch from the shelf by the front door before she left.

She pulled on her pyjamas over her T-shirt and jeans, took the thick fleece that Ruth had bought her from her drawer and climbed into bed. She hugged the fleece against her chest, rested her toes against the bulging bag. She could doze until Sunni came to bed. After that, she would need to make sure she stayed awake until everyone else was lost in sleep.

Addie stood in the moonlit yard. She waited, watched for light to appear in the windows of the dark house behind her; listened for footfalls and anxious voices behind the softly closed door. She hardly dared to breathe.

There was nothing. Just the hoot of a nearby owl and the faint, answering call of another from the trees behind the barn. It had been easier than Addie had expected to escape the sleeping house. Guilt prickled again: Ruth and Sam had come to trust her. She was breaking that trust.

She had to if the foal was ever to see his mam again.

Gabe had been right about the full moon. It stared down at Addie from high above the house, lit the edges of buildings and trees as if to encourage Addie on her way, threw black shapes across the yard to hide her. Addie crept towards the barn, grateful for the protective shadows.

The foal was sleepy, docile in the darkness. He lifted his head from his straw bed and sniffed at the piece of carrot Addie offered him. He looked at Addie, his head on one side. His eyes glimmered in the beam of Sam's torch.

'It's OK,' Addie said. 'I know it's not morning. But we've got somewhere to go . . .'

The foal stumbled to his feet, took the carrot from Addie's hand. His lips were warm and soft against her skin. His jaw slid from side to side, his crunching too loud in the silent barn. Addie fastened his head collar and led him into the night.

She couldn't use the quickest route on to the road she needed. She didn't dare risk the clatter of the foal's hooves near the farmhouse. She would cut behind the lambing shed and across the fields beyond Jude's treehouse. She felt for the makeshift map in the pocket of her jeans, switched Sam's torch to its lowest beam and studied the notes she had made from the laptop.

Winsford Moor first, then down the hill to Withypool Common – unless the foal had already found his mam among the Winsford ponies. She *had* to be among one of those herds. According to Gabe, they were the only herds anywhere near the spot where the little guy had been found, all alone in the snow.

'Come on,' she whispered to him. 'This way. After Jude's meadow, we just have to follow the bridleway signs: the blue ones, not the yellow ones, otherwise it won't be easy ground for you to manage.'

Blue. Mam's favourite colour. Addie felt the brush of her presence beside her in the lonely night. What would she say if she knew where Addie was right now?

There was an eerie stillness in the meadow without the daytime hum of insects and the song of the birds that nested in the oaks and evergreens. The mother birds would be there, though, Addie knew, huddled down low in their homes of feather and twig, protecting their young from the chill night air.

Jude's tree stood silhouetted against the moon, which seemed to hang lower in the sky here. Addie stopped, stared up at the moon's bright face. Perhaps, wherever Mam was, she was looking at it too. And thinking of Addie. Missing her.

The foal nudged her arm.

'Yes,' Addie said. 'Sorry. Let's go and find *your* mam.'

She looked back over her shoulder. No one was

following. She adjusted the heavy bag on her shoulder, rested her arm across the foal's warm neck and urged him forward towards the gate at the far end of the meadow.

It wouldn't open. Wild grass, grown high in the last few days of rain, was entwined around the hinges. Great clumps of it had sprouted round it, preventing it from swinging free. Why did everything have to be so difficult?

Addie tugged at the tough blades of grass, freed some of the strong roots from the muddy ground. Her hands stung. She should have worn her gloves as well as her new boots. She wiped her palms on her coat.

She managed to move the gate forward a little, but had to give the foal more carrot and a mint from her bag to persuade him through the narrow gap she had created.

Once through the gate, progress was still slow. The central track across the field was lined with dense gorse. It snatched at Addie's clothes and seemed to be an irresistible delicacy for the foal. He wandered along; stopped frequently to nibble at the prickly branches, tore at the yellow flowers clustered along them.

'How come you can eat that stuff?' Addie said. She

freed her coat sleeve from the clutches of a particularly vicious branch and clicked her tongue to urge the foal onwards. At this rate, it would be morning before they were anywhere near either of the herds.

'Come on,' she said. 'You've got to go much quicker if you want to find your mam before someone finds *us*. You *can't* be hungry any more!'

The first of the blue signs was hidden among gorse and bramble bushes at a fork in the track. Addie almost missed it. If her hand-drawn map was right, the right fork would lead them through a wooden gate and take them on to a proper road for a while.

It did. The foal picked up speed on the tarmac surface. His hooves echoed loudly. But there was no one to hear other than a small, quick creature that darted in front of Addie, and the owls that continued to call, perhaps reporting on the new visitors to their dark world.

The road seemed longer than it had looked on the website map, with more twists and turns. Addie wondered if it was the wrong one after all, or if they had missed the next blue sign along the way.

She was thirsty. She stopped and drank from her water bottle. She poured a little into her cupped hand for the foal. He nosed at it, began to drink.

He threw back his head, startled by a snap of twigs and rustle of leaves nearby. The bottle flew from Addie's hand, rolled to the side of the road, disappeared into the deep, dark ditch that ran alongside it.

'That's it then,' Addie said. 'No more water now. Better hope we find your mam soon.'

The rustle came again, closer this time, louder.

Addie flicked on the torch. She swung the beam in the direction of the sound. Bright eyes gleamed red from the hedgerow. There was a flash of white tooth and claw. Addie glimpsed shadowy, striped fur. She backed away, let the beam fall away from the staring eyes. What kind of creature was this? An image of Sunni's fearsome cat flitted through her mind. But that was just a story. This was most likely a badger, she thought, out hunting for food. Gabe said badgers were pretty fierce, especially at this time of year, when they were rearing their cubs. Should she keep still, or move further away? Her heartbeat sounded in her ears. Surely the creature could hear it, too?

The foal whinnied, pulled away from the hedge. The rustle became a frantic scuffle, another flash of white, a splinter of branches.

Addie swung the torch beam in a wide loop. She let out a long breath. 'I think it's gone,' she whispered to the foal. 'Whatever it was, you frightened it away.'

They walked on. Addie kept the torch on, swept the beam from side to side as they moved, checking for eyes and teeth, anxious to find the missing blue sign. The road narrowed, became steeper. Addie felt clammy in her thick coat despite a new chill in the air.

Round the next bend, staggered rooftops loomed grey above the trees: a farm – Highcroft, or something. Addie remembered it from the map. It stood on the edge of Winsford Moor. And there, to the left, was the blue sign, fixed to a low metal gate. She hadn't missed it after all.

This gate opened easily, on silent hinges. This time, the foal hurried through, head held high. His pale nostrils flared.

Addie pointed ahead. 'Winsford Moor,' she said. 'Just over there.' She pressed her face against the foal's face. His lashes brushed her cheek. 'Is that your home?'

The foal's ears twitched, stiffened. Addie pulled away, looked into his eyes. 'What can you hear?' she asked. 'Is it them? Is it the herd?'

The foal scraped at the ground; sniffed the air.

Addie swallowed past the lump in her throat. Was she about to say goodbye to him? She ran her hand down his velvet nose; felt his weight shift towards her for a moment, then move away. His neck stretched forward.

'Right,' Addie said. 'Let's go and see.'

TWENTY-FIVE

The moorland heather was grey in the moonlight; stiff and scratchy against Addie's jeans. She stumbled as she tried to keep pace with the foal. He seemed to have no problem with the tangle of undergrowth, or the rise and fall of the ground on this part of the moor.

The air was cooler now. It draped damp fingers across Addie's skin. The moon had dimmed, its face hazy in a deep grey sky. Addie shivered. She squinted, scanned the fading landscape. Where exactly *were* they? If they were crossing the moor in the right direction – towards Tarr Steps – they should be going downhill by now. She'd made a mistake somehow. There was no sign of the Winsford Hill herd, with their brown, dun or bay coats; no sign of any wild ponies at all.

She needed to catch her breath, get her bearings again. She stopped and slung her bag down among the heather-strewn bracken. The foal strained against the leading rein. He stared at Addie, then threw his head from side to side. His eyes flashed under their pale lids.

'I know,' she said. 'You're getting excited now. You want to get to your mam.' The foal nodded, blew through his nostrils. 'But just wait a minute.' She slid her fingers under his head collar. His fur was damp, his breath warm on her skin. 'I need to work out what to do next.'

Addie took her crumpled map from her pocket, tried to make sense of her drawing in the wavering beam of the torch while hanging on to the foal. She couldn't match it to the landscape any more; couldn't make it fit with the sweep of grey moorland that stretched in every direction, rising and falling to reveal dark hills beyond.

She wasn't very good at drawing maps. It was useless now, anyway. She scrunched it into a ball and threw it down among the heather. They were lost.

The foal was straining to move on. Perhaps he had more idea of where they were going than Addie did. She picked up her bag and let him lead her forward.

The ground became gradually steeper, slowing their progress. The foal stopped every few yards now. He tossed his head. He froze for several moments before walking on. The hair on his back bristled under Addie's hand. What had he sensed? Was it the herd – or something else?

Something Addie didn't want to find.

The air was thick now, almost opaque: as if the rising ground had taken Addie and the foal into the sky; into a cloud. Addie could barely see where to put her feet. The torch was next to useless, its beam nothing more than a pale, spreading halo around her hand.

Mist.

A moorland mist.

Addie had heard about those: the sudden white blankets that stilled and silenced the great moor for hours at a time, stole the land and the sky. Stole people. Her neck prickled inside the collar of her coat. What if Sunni's Big Cat Beast was real after all, lurking out there, waiting for the mist to thicken? Waiting to pounce.

She thought of the skinny cats at home scurrying across the dark streets, slipping between the houses, their eyes like tiny lamps in the night. Sunni's Big Cat would have no trouble spotting Addie and the foal, even in this mist. But by the time *they* saw him, it would be too late . . .

'*Stop it!*' she told herself. There *was* no Big Cat; no Beast of Exmoor. It was just Sunni and her nonsense;

just a story. She reached for the foal, wriggled her fingers through his wiry mane. 'We'll be all right,' she whispered. 'You and me together. This mist can't last long. It must be nearly morning. We'll stay here and keep each other warm.'

Addie's body ached and her eyes stung with tiredness. She longed to sit down. Dare she try to rest among the springy heather? Images of the vivid snakes she had seen on Ruth's laptop came to mind. She imagined their dry bodies squirming unseen around her in the mist, winding over her as she slept.

There would be other creatures, too . . . She would have to stay on her feet.

She leaned close to the foal's warm flank and forced herself to eat some bread and cheese from her bag. She offered the foal some apple and a sugar lump for energy. He wouldn't take either. He shifted from one foot to the other. The hair on his back stood in stiff clumps now. He swung his head away; swung it back. The muscles in his neck moved like strong ropes under Addie's hands as she tried to soothe him.

'It's OK,' she whispered. 'Everything's OK.'

But someone – some*thing* – was coming. The foal sensed it. And so did Addie.

She felt it in the ground at first: a rhythmic rumble, pulsing through her from beneath her feet. Her heartbeat joined the rhythm, fast and hard. What was happening?

Sound came next: a great rolling, pounding wave of sound that filled her ears, filled her body. The ground shook and vibrated. The foal's body quivered against Addie's side.

Addie gripped his head collar; buried her face in his neck. The shaking and pounding grew stronger. Addie felt as if her ears might burst. She couldn't move.

The foal flung back his head, throwing Addie's arms from his neck. He whinnied: a long, shrill note that Addie had never heard before – yet knew, somewhere deep inside herself.

Then she saw them: dark eyes looming from the white air, dark manes streaming, hooves flashing as they thundered towards her. The flow of dark bodies seemed to float; to rise and fall like merry-go-round horses in the mist. Addie stared; could not look away. She felt herself lifting into the air beside them . . .

The foal called again – louder this time.

Addie blinked and rubbed at her eyes. 'Is this your family?' she shouted. 'Has your mam come? Has she?'

Her words were whisked away with the rush and roar of the galloping herd.

The foal turned towards Addie. His eyes glinted: bright specks of light in the misted air. He rested his head on her shoulder for a moment. His muzzle brushed velvet-soft against her cheek. Addie stroked his back. A new heat rose through his skin. Addie felt the race of his heart beneath. Or perhaps it was her own heart. She couldn't tell.

She cupped her hand round his ear. 'It's OK,' she whispered. 'I know you have to go.' She felt for the buckles on his halter and slid the straps down over his ears and nose.

The foal tossed his head, registering his freedom. His front legs lifted and then he was still again. Addie kissed his nose, breathed in the scent of him one last time. She stepped backwards.

'Go on,' she shouted. 'Go and see your mam!'

The foal froze for a moment, then twisted away from Addie. His tail whipped high against her chest. His hooves scrabbled for purchase, stirring the damp earth beneath the heather. A musty scent rose into the air.

And then he was gone. Stolen from sight by mist and dust and the disappearing dark river of ponies.

Addie stared after them until the moor fell silent. Her blood thundered in her ears. A deep pain tugged at her chest, pulled at her to run, to follow. To fly with the herd and to rest with them in their forest home. To have their warm bodies encircle her, keeping her from harm.

Keeping *them* from harm. Addie and her foal.

An invisible tether connected the two of them now; threaded its way back through the trees, through the mist, through to the very middle of Addie from the brown brick house. Would it break when she left the moor without him?

Would *she*?

Her legs were trembling now. They would no longer hold her up. She sank down among the spiky stems and springy heather. She balanced her bag on her knees, rested her chin there. Let the snakes come. She didn't care any more. She squeezed her eyes shut and tried to block out the lonely moor; the snakebite pain of knowing that the foal was gone.

That she was alone.

Again.

The warmth of tears surprised her. She wiped them away. She *wouldn't* cry.

She should be happy. She'd done what she set out to do. The foal was home.

A soft shadow shifted close by. Addie heard the brush of gorse. Was it him? Had the foal changed his mind and come back to her? She twisted round; tried to see. She struggled to stand. Could not. What was wrong with her legs?

'I'm still here,' she shouted. 'Over here. Here!' She squinted in the direction of the sound; listened for the soft thud of hooves that she knew so well; the answering call in the blank air.

There was nothing.

Only silence. Held-breath silence.

It wasn't him.

Of course it wasn't him.

Addie wrapped her arms round herself, tried to stop the trembling that now rose up through her legs and into her chest and throat.

Something was there, though.

Something was close.

Something that wasn't the foal . . .

A snap of twigs behind her now.

She should move.

Hide.

But how?

Where?

She couldn't even see her own hands now. She couldn't move.

The mist seemed to solidify around her, binding her to the silent moor. Holding her there. She was cold. Ice-cold. Frozen. Her teeth rattled together. Would Sam find her here tomorrow? Here, among the heather, stiff and still, like the clay people waiting for her in the silence of the brown brick house.

Another sound, barely there: a shuddering of air.

Addie was done for.

Sam would find no trace of her. Sunni would whisper her name in tales of mysterious moorland beasts and merciless mists.

Would anyone even miss her?

TWENTY-SIX

The mist swirled around Addie, seeped into her mind, began to steal her away, piece by piece. Away from the white wilderness and the wild beast biding its time behind her. Away from Oaktree Farm with its wide open skies, from Jude and his flowers, from Gabe with his grim jokes, his ridiculous hats; his big-brother eyes.

Away from the foal who had been her friend.

There was nothing now. Nothing but the empty bridge by the river, the empty brown brick house, the empty girl that used to be Addie.

And Mam, who made promises she didn't keep.

Addie's eyes sprang open.

Mam.

What would happen to Mam if Addie didn't make it off the moor?

She was ill. That's what Penny and Ruth said. And she was trying her hardest to get well.

Addie could *never* forget *her*.

She needed to get herself together. She listened.

All was quiet. Just a slight rustle of wind across the heather. It lifted strands of Addie's hair now. Perhaps it would blow away the mist.

How long had she been sitting here? The beast would have sprung by now, if it was going to. If it was there. Surely.

Anyway, she *had* to get up. Beast or no beast.

She *had* to keep moving.

Addie rubbed at her arms and legs, trying to bring some life back into them, and hauled herself to her feet.

Her legs were stiff and slow. They still trembled with every step. She thought of the foal, wobbling on his thin legs when he first came to the farm. Pain stabbed at her chest again. She took a deep breath and edged slowly forward, arms outstretched as if this were a game of blind man's bluff. Maybe it would help to pretend that it was. Addie was good at pretending.

It didn't help.

The rough ground was more of a challenge without the foal beside her; the blurred air more unnerving now that she was alone. She could find herself rolling down a hill, tangling with a snake, or in the claws of that Big Cat at any moment. Her throat was dust-dry.

She should have taken more care of the water, brought more supplies.

She remembered Ruth's cookies and felt around in her bag for them. She stood still and ate them all to keep her going, even though it was hard to swallow and she thought she might be sick. She tried to conjure the warmth of the farmhouse kitchen: remembered Ruth – the softness in her eyes. What would she do when she discovered that Addie was not in her bed? Would she call Penny? Would Penny tell Mam?

Addie stumbled forward, inching her way in the direction she hoped might being her to the brow of a hill. A bird called – shrill and loud – as if to warn of Addie's arrival in its territory. If Addie remembered correctly, the walk downhill would take her into some woods, bring her to a river and to Tarr Steps, with its tourist café and car parks. There would be no Big Cat and no snakes there, she felt sure. She would be safe until morning, when there should be a bus to take her close to the farm.

She could only hope that she was heading in the right direction . . .

The river shivered in the low light; glinted black, silver and green as it gurgled over grey stones. Slender trees leaned across it, their branches and new leaves forming a canopy overhead. Others bent low, branches spreading in the water like dark, twisted fingers. There was an eerie yellow glow where the light touched them.

Addie tightened the drawstring of her hood. It was colder here, despite the shelter of the trees. Remnants of mist hung in mid-air and drifted over the water like small clouds. Addie watched them go; thought of the foal disappearing into the herd. By now he would be back with his mother, snuggled up, safe and warm. Back where he belonged.

Perhaps he had already forgotten Addie and Jude, and Oaktree Farm.

Addie shivered, like the river water. She needed to find the bridge and get herself somewhere warm for a while.

But then, perhaps she *shouldn't* hurry too much to get back to the farm after all. If she wasn't back by early morning, they'd have to tell Mam that she was missing, wouldn't they? They'd have to.

When they did, Mam would come running to find her.

And she'd never let Addie out of her sight again.

The Tarr Steps bridge was very old. Nothing more

than a line of giant grey stones, flattened and worn by the millions of feet that must have walked across them over the centuries. Great slabs had been propped up alongside the footway, as if to stop it from drifting downstream. The river water was high after all the rain and lapped over it in places. Addie didn't think any of it looked very safe. But she needed to get across.

She stepped on to the first stone. It was slimy and slippery underfoot. Addie wished there was something to hold on to for balance. She was glad of the new boots that Ruth had bought her, with their chunky ridged soles and high tops.

She peered into the water and tried to work out how deep it was. Her face stared back, fractured and trembling on the surface of the river.

When she looked up again, she was no longer alone.

TWENTY-SEVEN

Flo stood on the other end of the bridge, her amber eyes fixed on Addie, her white-tipped tail held high. Water flowed over her paws.

'Flo! What are you doing here?'

The dog ran towards Addie, her steps quick and sure on the wet stones. She licked Addie's hand with her rough tongue, turned and stared back towards the riverbank. She gave four sharp barks, waited; gave another four: louder this time.

Who was she calling to? Gabe?

Whoever it was, Addie thought, must be looking for *her*. Her disappearance from the farm had been noticed.

It wasn't Gabe.

It was Sunni – an explosion of colour among the trees and bushes in her purple coat and Ruth's scarlet scarf.

No! Not *Sunni*.

They faced one another from either end of the bridge. Neither of them moved. Flo ran backwards and forwards between them, pink tongue lolling from the side of her mouth.

'No foal, then?' Sunni shouted. 'I knew you were crazy.' She clutched at her head. 'But I can't believe you've actually done this.'

'Mind your own business,' Addie shouted back. 'Go away.'

Sunni glanced back over her shoulder. 'You've got to come back to the farm. Right *now*,' she yelled.

'Or what?' Addie said. 'Go away, Sunni.'

'You've *got* to. Come on,' Sunni yelled. She grabbed a twig from the edge of the river and threw it towards Addie.

Flo jumped up and snatched the twig from the air. She collided with Addie and careered over the leaning stone barrier, into the river. Addie tottered, almost fell in with her. She steadied herself and watched Flo's black and white head bob above the surface as she swam easily through the dark water.

Addie wasn't staying on the bridge.

She stepped on to the bank next to Sunni, careful to avoid her accusing gaze. Flo landed beside them; shook herself dry in a blur of water droplets and green algae.

Sunni brushed at the bottom of her coat. She pointed

ahead, where the ground dropped downhill through the trees. 'This way,' she said. 'It's quickest. Your map was wrong.'

Addie stared at her. She looked different. Her smug smile was missing. Her face seemed thinner, her golden skin tighter over her sharp bones. '*What*?' she said.

'Flo found it,' Sunni said, 'back there in the heather.' She reached towards the dog, smoothed her back. 'Best sniffer dog *and* best sheepdog ever, aren't you, Flo?'

'What, you've been following me?'

Sunni shook her head. 'We need to go now,' she said.

Addie was going nowhere. Not until she had some answers. 'Well. Have you?'

'Jude. All right? Jude told me. He got scared; thought you might need some help. He woke me up.'

'He didn't really know where I was going,' Addie said. 'I didn't get chance to say.'

Sunni shrugged. 'That was the easy bit – you'd have to be heading for Winsford and Withypool. Obviously.' Her usual smirk crept back across her face. 'But you took the long way round. I nearly gave up.' The smirk fell away. Her lips twisted into something like a snarl. 'Pity your mam didn't teach you to draw maps instead of flowers.'

Addie couldn't look at Sunni for a moment longer. 'Shut up,' she said. 'I don't need help,' she said. 'Not from you and not from anybody else.' She patted Flo's head. 'See you later, girl.'

She threw her bag over her shoulder and set off in the direction that Sunni had indicated. It *was* the right way, as far as she could remember, without her stupid map to help her.

Sunni grabbed her arm from behind, her fingers needle-sharp through Addie's sleeve.

Addie spun round to face her. Her shoulder bag swung against Sunni's chest. 'Get off, idiot,' she said, her teeth clenched tight. 'I'll be back when I'm ready. Leave me alone.'

'It's not about you, though,' Sunni said. She pushed her face close to Addie's. 'It's about Ruth. And Sam. Only you're much too selfish to think about *them*.'

Addie let her bag fall to the ground; jammed her hands on to her hips. 'You've told them, haven't you? Bet you loved that – getting me into trouble.' She held her hand over her eyes and peered through the trees. 'So where are they then? Ruth and Sam? Waiting in the car park to take me to the police station, where I belong?'

Sunni looked away. She shook her head. 'I haven't told, OK?' She chewed at her lower lip. 'Well, I left a note for Gabe. Just in case. In his beanie hat. I said we'd borrowed Flo for some early-morning sheepdog practice.'

Addie stared at her. 'What? Why?'

'You don't get it, do you?' Sunni said. 'You're too obsessed with your precious foal and your precious *mam* to think about anyone at the farm!'

'Maybe you would care about *your* mam a bit more if she even *liked* you,' Addie said.

Sunni blinked, looked away into the distance. Her shoulders sagged, lifted again. When she looked back, her chin was tilted high and the black line around one eye was smudged on to her cheek.

Addie bit her lip. She shouldn't have said that. Not even to Sunni.

'Sorry,' she said. 'I didn't mean –'

'I don't care what you think,' Sunni said. Her eyes were narrow now – fierce, like the eyes of the wild badger hiding in the hedge. 'I only care about what will happen to Ruth and Sam if the Social find out you've gone off in the middle of the night – in a mist – when they're supposed to be looking after you.'

Something splashed in the water behind them. Addie looked back, grateful for a distraction from the sharp sting of Sunni's words. She caught a glimpse of a thin brown tail among a cluster of twisted roots and broken branches close to the bank.

Sunni slumped down on a tree stump. 'Otter, most likely,' she said, her voice flat, tired. 'There's loads of them round here.' She sighed. 'Can we fight later?' she said. 'Please, Addie, we have to get back before Sam finishes milking. He'll call out Search and Rescue and there'll be even worse trouble . . .'

Sunni never said please. What was going on? Addie didn't trust her. She threw down her bag and sat on it. 'How come you're so bothered about Ruth and Sam? I mean, they're nice and everything, but –'

'But what?' Sunni said.

Addie picked at a patch of moss at the base of Sunni's seat. It was damp and springy under her fingers. 'Well, they're not your family, are they? They just look after you, like for a job. They do it for money. That's all.' Her throat tightened. Why had she said that? It wasn't true. She knew it wasn't.

Sunni jumped to her feet. 'You are the stupidest person I've ever met in my whole life,' she shouted.

'Serves you right if your social worker puts you somewhere really horrible next.'

Flo barked, circled around Sunni's feet, looked from her to Addie and back again.

'Next?' Addie said. She crossed her fingers behind her back. 'There won't be a "next". Mam's nearly better. I'm going home.'

Sunni raised her eyebrows. 'Think you're so clever, don't you? Out here by yourself, taking the foal back to his mum and everything? Well, tell yourself that tomorrow, when you're locked up in a children's home with someone's beady eye on you the whole time so you can't do a disappearing act.'

Addie felt hot. Blistering hot. She clenched her fists; dug her nails into her palms. She *really* hated Sunni.

Sunni grabbed Flo's collar. 'Come on, Flo,' she said. 'We're going.' Her voice wavered; she was actually crying.

'Don't know why you're crying,' Addie said. She stood up and stepped close to Sunni. She felt her breath, soft on her own cheek. 'You should be happy. If I do get taken away, you'll get Ruth and Sam's attention back on you again. You'll have your stupid room with your stupid elephants all to yourself again. You'll be able to keep pretending that you're staying at the farm because you actually want to, and not because your mam's got a new baby that she likes better than she likes you!'

There, she'd said it now. The words hung in the air between them. Addie's stomach clenched.

Sunni was staring at her. Her mouth opened and closed again. She turned away. Her shoulders shook under her purple coat.

Guilty tears pushed at Addie's eyes. What had happened to her? Where had she gone? Another Addie had taken her place. This one was no better than Darren Oates.

She grabbed hold of Sunni's hand.

'What did you mean?' she asked. 'About Ruth and Sam – what's going to happen to them?'

'Not just them. All of us.' Sunni glared at Addie, her eyes darker than the river water. 'You think the Social will still let them be foster parents when they've lost you – twice?' She tore her arm free from Addie's hand. Her eyes filled, overflowed. 'You want to get home. Good for you. Go on then. I hope your precious *mam* remembers you're there this time. But what about Jude? What about me? What about all the other kids who need to come here . . .?' She wiped her arm across her face, made dark streaks on her purple sleeve. 'You're so sorry for yourself,

Addie; you think you're so special – like you're the only one in the world who had bad stuff happen to them.' She drew in a broken breath, let it out again. She pushed back her shoulders. 'Oaktree Farm – with Ruth and Sam and Gabe: it's where I *live* now. It's my *home*. And it was going to be to be forever.' Her voice rose loud and high; landed in the centre of Addie like a punch. 'And now *you're* taking it away from me.'

Sunni turned away, stalked back among the trees with Flo at her heels.

Even the dog didn't like Addie any more.

A chorus of birdsong broke out above, panicked and shrill. Addie looked up into the thick canopy of leaves overhead. She could barely see the sky.

Her legs felt as if they were made of rubber.

What had she done? She hadn't meant to ruin things for anyone at the farm. She'd just wanted to make things right for the foal.

Well, he was happy now. He was home. All because of her.

But if Sunni and Jude lost *their* home, that would be because of her too.

She sank to her knees. Beside her, honeysuckle twisted strong and green round a tree trunk, waited for the summer sunshine to unfurl its flowers. Pink, purple and white starflowers. Like the ones in Mam's last painting.

Addie covered her face with her hands; longed for the warm presence of the foal beside her. Everything was worse than ever.

Was it too late to put some of it right?

She struggled to her feet. She had to hurry, had to catch up with Sunni.

She would *not* miss that early bus back to the farm...

TWENTY-EIGHT

Jude shuffled back against the wall of the treehouse. Sunlight winked in the mirrored fabric above his head and picked out the pink spots on his cheeks and hands. He pulled his knees up under his chin. 'What does she look like, the foal's mum?'

'I told you,' Addie said, 'there were loads of ponies. A whole herd, probably. I didn't see his actual mam.'

'But *the foal* saw her, though?'

'Maybe. Or else he knew the others would take him to her.'

'His brothers and everything?'

Addie nodded. She picked up a shrivelled leaf from the floor. It was paper-thin, its skeleton of life-giving veins still visible. She held it high; let it drop. It drifted for a second in the draught from the entrance and was still.

Jude screwed up his eyes, as if trying to picture everything Addie had told him. 'Wish I saw the herd too,' he said.

'I know,' Addie said. 'But our foal's happy now, isn't he? That's the main thing.'

Jude brushed dust from his shoe. 'Sunni says you're in trouble and Penny's got to take you away,' he said. He looked up at her, his brow wrinkled. 'She says you got Ruth and Sam in trouble too.'

Tears prickled behind Addie's eyes. She willed them not to fall. 'Sunni doesn't know anything,' she said, shaking her head. And anyway, she made things a million times worse all by herself. She should have guessed Gabe would go all grown up and tell, when he found her stupid note in his hat. If it wasn't for that, we'd have been safely back from the moor before Ruth and Sam discovered we were missing. They wouldn't have had to call the Social in a panic and *Addie* would be the only one in trouble.

Jude leaned forward towards her. 'I told *my* social worker that it was my plan too,' he said. 'About the foal. I said he's got to take me away as well. With you. Cos that's fair.' He gave a quick nod of his head. His hair fell across his eyes.

Addie thought of Ruth sitting beside Jude on the kitchen floor that first morning, knowing what to do; knowing what *not* to do to help him. She thought of Jude nestled among his primroses, his face full of wonder and pride. She gazed around the hollow tree space that Sunni had made special for him.

The space where he still had a brother.

She shook her head. 'No, Jude,' she said. 'You're staying here. On the farm. OK? It's a good place. For you. Until you get back with Thomas.'

Jude rubbed at his eyes, pushed loose curls away from them. He traced circles in the dusty floor with his fingers. He looked up at Addie, one finger still moving.

'I *got* to go away, Addie.' His voice was a thin whisper. 'Tim said. And then I won't never see you or Ruth or Sunni again.'

Addie shuffled across the space between them, drew her knees up alongside Jude's. She tilted her head and rested it on his shoulder. He didn't move away.

'What? No, Jude,' she said. 'I'm the one that's in trouble and I'm the only one that might get sent away.'

They were all there now, in the kitchen – Penny, Ruth Sam and some man with a round face and a briefcase even bigger than Penny's – discussing things, deciding things. Like always.

'But if I do go somewhere else, Jude, you can ring me. OK? And you can send me drawings of your flowers – Ruth will help you . . .'

Jude shook his head, pulled away. He stared into Addie's eyes. 'It's not cos of you,' he said. 'Tim's found a f'rever family that wants me now. They choosed me.' His eyes swam and overflowed. 'But I want *here* to be my forever place,' he said, his voice almost too quiet for Addie to hear.

Addie stared back at him. 'What do you mean?'

Jude's shoulders lifted, fell. 'I'm getting adopted. Tim said.'

'When? What else did Tim say?'

Jude sniffed. 'He said . . . he said it's a f'rever family with two dads and a dog.'

Jude's eyes searched Addie's own. Addie hoped he couldn't see through them to the inside of her – to her spinning heart. So, she was going to lose Jude now too. Even if she got to stay at the farm.

She searched for a smile and found a small one. For Jude.

'You'll like having a dog of your own. It'll be fun. Liam Bell at my old school, his dads brought their dog to my last sports day. It ran down the track after Liam in the hundred-metre race. And it came second!'

Addie remembered other things about that day. Mam arriving too late to see her win first place in the hurdles; Mam hurrying towards her with someone else's smile sliding across her face; the clink and rattle of glass in her too-heavy handbag.

'Did your mum come as well?' Jude asked. 'To the sports day?'

Addie shook her head. 'No,' she said. 'She forgot.'

'Like my mum and dad forgetted about me and Thomas?' Jude said. Some of the old darkness crept across his eyes.

Addie swallowed hard. 'Yes,' she said. 'Maybe.'

'Ruth doesn't forget about us, does she?'

'No,' Addie said, 'she doesn't.'

Jude's face crumpled 'What if my new dads do, though?' Tears wobbled in the corners of his eyes.

Addie rummaged in her pocket for a tissue. She didn't have one. Just Mam's shell, nestled at the bottom. It was warm, as if there might still be something living, breathing, inside it. She closed her palm gently round it.

'They won't forget you, Jude,' she said. 'They chose you specially, didn't they? And anyway, Tim and Ruth wouldn't let them take you if they might do that.'

'Promise?'

'Promise.'

Jude wiped his sleeve across his face. 'Tim said my

new dads have got a comfy house with a room specially for me. And a big garden.' A flicker of light danced across his eyes. 'With lots and lots of flowers in it. *And* a treehouse. A high-up one.'

Dust caught in Addie's throat; tried to steal her voice.

Mam. The Foal. Now Jude.

A door slammed shut in her chest.

What was the point in loving people when they always had to leave?

She tightened her fingers round Mam's shell. Something sharp snatched at her skin. She pulled the shell from her pocket. A tiny piece had come loose, leaving a sharp, ragged edge. A bright bubble of blood appeared on Addie's thumb. It widened and trickled down, deep inside the pink hollow that had once been someone's home.

Addie wiped her thumb on her jeans, pushed the broken shell back into her pocket. 'I've got to go, Jude. Penny's waiting for me,' she said. She scrambled out of the treehouse and ran across the meadow towards the farm.

She might as well find out where Penny was going to send her right now.

It didn't really matter any more.

TWENTY-NINE

They were still sitting round the table – Penny, Ruth and the round-faced man – papers and pens strewn among coffee mugs in front of them. There was a plate of Ruth's scones. It didn't look as if anyone had eaten one.

Penny was smiling. But that didn't mean anything good. Social workers always smiled. They did it to make themselves feel better about doing things that upset people. A wave of ice ran across Addie's skin in the warmth of the kitchen doorway.

'Addie, come on in and sit down, sweetheart.' Ruth patted the seat next to her. 'I was just about to come and get you.'

Addie didn't move.

The man turned his chair towards Addie. He was smiling too. 'That's OK. You stay there if you'd rather, Addie.'

Addie put her hands in her pockets. She lifted her chin and looked into the man's face. She couldn't remember his name. He tilted his head to one side like one of the owls that roosted in the barns. His smile became wider; soft at the edges. Addie saw it flash in his eyes behind his large glasses.

'Addie,' he said, 'Penny and I have thought very hard about what you told us, and we've had a good chat with Ruth. So, now we –'

'If you think I care about getting sent somewhere else, I don't! OK? Take me anywhere you want.' Addie pushed back her shoulders, tried to steady the tremble in her hands. 'But Ruth and Sam haven't done anything wrong. It was all me. You've got to let them keep Jude and Sunni, and let other children come here. And if you don't, I'll just keep running away. Wherever you put me. I'll be the worst trouble you've ever had to deal with.'

The owl man's smile slid away. His eyes crinkled at the edges. His forehead creased. He nodded slowly.

'It's OK, Addie,' he said. 'I understand. We all do. And there's no need to be scared. His voice rose and fell like a song. 'First of all, Ruth and Sam aren't in any trouble. Nobody is being taken anywhere at the moment. OK? We do need to talk about things here; ensure you stay safe here in future, but just so you stop worrying –'

Addie glanced at Ruth, who nodded, offered her a reassuring smile.

Addie sank on to the nearest chair. 'Good,' she said, her voice suddenly small. She would say sorry to Ruth and Sam. Later. She might even say sorry to Sunni. But only for worrying them all. Not for stealing the foal away; for getting him home. She wasn't sorry for that.

She pulled her shoulders back, sat up tall in her chair. 'I wasn't scared,' she told the owl man. 'And I'm still worried. About my mam.' She shot an angry look in Penny's direction. 'No one ever understands about *that*. When am I seeing her?'

'What we all want for you,' the owl man said, 'is to get you and your mum back together as soon as possible. That's what you want too, I know –'

'We should be together now,' she said. 'I keep telling *her*.' She pointed at Penny. 'Mam needs me. She can't get better without me.' Hot tears pressed behind her eyes again. She blinked them back.

Penny stood up, pulled her own chair across the floor towards Addie. Its legs screeched on the tiles. 'Well,' she said, 'there *is* some good news about your mum, Addie.'

The kitchen seemed brighter. Too bright. Addie

blinked again, looked at Penny, at Ruth. At the owl man. The clock ticked more loudly than usual

'What?' she asked. 'What then? Is Mam OK now? When can I go home?'

'Not just yet, Addie, I'm afraid,' Penny said. 'But your mum is doing much better, sweetheart. There's been a big change in her recently.'

Addie stared at Penny. 'So she *is* better, then?'

'Better than she was, yes, Addie. But not better enough for you to go home yet.'

Addie's nails dug into her palms. Her breath was loud in her ears. There *wasn't* any good news. There never was.

Penny took hold of Addie's fists. Her fingers were cool and gentle. Like Mam's used to be. Addie wanted to pull her hands away. She didn't.

'Addie, getting better – better enough to be your mum again – well, that's really, really hard. Remember what I told you?'

Addie looked at Penny out of the corners of her eyes; moved a little further inside herself.

Penny shuffled on to the edge of her chair. 'It's been so difficult for your mum, Addie, trying to manage without drinking. She thought the drink was her friend;

that it helped her when she was worried, or lonely. But it didn't. It made her unwell. And it stopped her being herself, didn't it?'

'It's not *her* fault,' Addie said.

'No. But what happened made you very sad, I know. And it made your mum sad too.'

Penny's hands grew warmer round Addie's. The owl man cleared his throat. Addie heard the kettle being filled by Ruth.

'Your mum's very brave. Like you are, Addie,' Penny said. 'And she loves you very much. But getting well is a long fight for her. And she can't win every battle. Sometimes, she loses. That's what happened the day you were going to meet up at the café. But she's been winning for a while now. And the *good* news is that the team think she'll be ready to go home in another month. And –'

'Why can't I see her then? You said I'd see her ages ago!'

The owl man leaned forward, his elbows on his knees. 'Addie, your mum wants to see you, too. Very badly. And Penny has tried to arrange something with her. But your mum wants to be sure that she's ready. She knows that she let you down and she doesn't want that to happen again. She wants to see how she gets on at home by herself for a bit first. With some help from us. And she's right. It's important that she does that. None of us want things go back to how they were, do we?'

Addie looked at his kind face. She thought of the bottles under the table and under Mam's bed. Remembered the empty fridge. The ache of her empty stomach when she tried to sleep at night.

She remembered Mam's empty eyes.

Addie didn't like those things about home.

She turned away. The owl man wasn't going to see her cry.

The fridge children grinned at her from the corner of the room.

As if they knew her.

As if she was just like them.

Their faces blurred. Addie squeezed her eyes shut. She searched for the crawl space inside herself where none of this was happening. She slid to the floor, her head heavy on her knees.

She sensed movement and felt someone settle close by.

A soft voice crept into the crawl space alongside her.

Ruth. 'Let's take a break, David,' she said. 'I think Addie needs some quiet time just now.'

❄ ❄ ❄

Addie curled up on the window seat. She clutched the mug of chocolate that Ruth had made for her. She watched Penny and Ruth talking to the owl man – David, or whatever his name was – in the yard. Their voices lifted and fell like chattering chickens. What were they saying now?

Ruth turned towards the window, spotted Addie, smiled and waved. 'Back in a mo,' she mouthed.

Addie wanted to smile back but her mouth stayed stiff and still.

She wasn't going to a children's home. Ruth and Sam weren't in trouble because of her. She hadn't ruined things for Sunni and Jude, or for anyone.

Mam *was* getting better.

Addie was glad. About all of it. But her body didn't seem to know that.

And now she didn't even have the foal to help her through.

On top of everything, she would have to start school here. In two weeks! Penny said it would be good for her. Ruth said it would be fine and 'the best thing'. But the best thing would be going back to Mam; back to the *old*

Mam; back to Addie's *old* school. She wanted to know when that would happen.

What if Mam wasn't well enough for her birthday in August?

How could she have her birthday without Mam?

The door opened. Flo appeared, panting. She made a dive for her water bowl and lapped noisily; thumped down at Addie's feet. Her gentle eyes sought Addie's face. Her feathered tail flicked up and down, just once, as if she knew that something was not quite right. Addie reached down and stroked her head. Flo nudged at her hand, wanting more. Just like the foal used to do.

Addie felt the foal beside her for a moment; felt his solid warmth and steady breath. His always being the same. His listening.

He was her best friend in the whole world. And she would never see him again. She might never see Jude again when he got adopted.

What if it was the same with Mam?

What if she *never* felt better enough for Addie to go home?

What then?

Addie wriggled Mam's shell from her pocket. It was cold now. She held it to her ear.

No more sea. No more lucky shell to take with her to the stupid new school. Just a stupid, broken, empty nothing.

She threw the shell to the floor: saw it fracture; fall apart. She wrapped her arms tightly round herself and tried to hold her splintered heart together.

Summer was nearly here, but Addie was cold to the bone.

THIRTY

It was a dazzling day; the sky a vivid blue banner over the farm.

'A special day for a special boy,' Ruth said, as she finished drying Jude's green cup. She put it in his backpack, along with the last of his things. She smiled at Jude, at Addie. Her hand rested on Addie's shoulder, feather soft and warm through Addie's T-shirt.

'They're here,' Sunni called from the kitchen window seat. She knocked on the glass. Waved. 'I'll tell them you're coming.' She jumped down, swung past Addie, and out into the hall. Anyone would think it was Sunni's day; Sunni's new dads arriving to take her to her forever home.

Addie looked across at Jude. His eyes were bright with tears; his cheeks flushed an excited pink. Like he couldn't decide whether he was happy or sad. He had hardly said a word since he got up.

Addie bent down, fiddled with the laces of her

trainers and tried to stop the quiver in her chin. She liked Jude's new parents, Paul and Rob. They seemed to love Jude already. They'd visited often. They'd taken Jude to buy seeds to plant behind the farmhouse: seeds that would grow into bright flowers every year, so that something of Jude would always be here on the farm.

They'd shown Addie their book of photographs. Pictures of their house, of Jude's room all decorated in green and yellow: primrose colours. Pictures of Jude's new silver-haired grandparents and of their funny, flat-faced dog called Fred. A picture of the treehouse Rob had built in the garden, especially for Jude. It had a proper roof, a red door and a strong ladder with rails to hold on to when you climbed up. Paul had said Addie could come and try it; could come for tea once Jude was settled. He had promised.

Ruth had promised too.

How long did settling take?

Addie wanted Paul and Rob to come in and eat Ruth's warm scones at the kitchen table. She wanted to push back the hands on the big kitchen clock, so that it would never be time for Jude to leave.

But Ruth had said that a long drawn-out goodbye

would be hardest for Jude. Today, Paul and Rob would just pop him in the car. And leave.

Addie pushed her mouth into a smile and stood up. 'Quick, Jude,' she said. 'Before Sunni goes and hides in the boot. She's dying to see your new house!'

Jude threw his arms round Ruth, who bent forward, held his face in her hands and smiled her gentle smile. 'Didn't you say something about a surprise for Addie and Sunni in your new car?' she asked.

Jude straightened up. His eyes widened. He nodded; sniffed. He heaved his backpack over one shoulder and pulled on Addie's sleeve.

'Come see,' he said.

They walked out into the courtyard together.

Paul was talking to Sam beside the car. Rob was leaning into the open boot. Sunni was trying to shoo a speckled hen out of the yard. It strutted around in circles, legs lifted high like a dancer. Its head flicked from side to side, back and forth. Sunni followed it, her arms spread wide.

'Hi there.' Paul waved, beamed at them both. 'Hi there, Jude! Hello, Addie.'

'Ah, Jude! Surprise time!' Rob lifted a square plastic box from the boot, steadied it against his chest. He slammed the boot shut. The hen squawked, flapped her short wings and scurried past him, out through the gate and on to the track. Addie watched her hurry on towards the safety of the henhouse.

'Sorry, hen,' Rob called after her. He bowed in apology. He smiled his wide smile. It made Addie smile too. Just for a moment.

Jude ran over to him. 'Show them,' he said. 'Show Addie and Sunni.' His smile was wide now, too: bright and real. Like Rob's.

Inside the box was a huge cake. A chocolate cake, with thick frosting on the top and sides. Jude's favourite.

'I helped make it, didn't I – Dad?' Jude turned to Paul, who had come over to stand beside him.

Paul nodded. His eyes glimmered in the sunlight: blue eyes, still as a lake. Like Jude's. Addie hadn't noticed that until now. She hadn't heard Jude call Paul 'Dad' before either. It made her feel funny inside: a mixture of happy and sad.

'You did help, Jude,' Paul said. 'You did most of the work! Best baker in town, I'd say.'

Jude puffed out his chest. An' I did the message all by myself,' he said. He pointed to the top of the cake, to words spelled out in loops of brightly coloured sweets.

I love you
From
JUDE.

He looked at Addie, at Sunni, across at Ruth and at Sam. Addie saw his small shoulders sink.

Paul saw it too. He darted forward and took Jude's hand. 'Lunch in your new treehouse today,' he said.

'Ooh, yes. And we've got some of Ruth's cookies for dessert,' Rob said. He rubbed his stomach. 'And Ruth's given us the recipe. So we can make some more whenever you want, Jude. How about that?'

Jude nodded. They walked together across the yard.

Addie watched Jude climb into the car. The shiny silver car that was taking him to his shiny forever life. His face appeared in the back window, golden behind the tinted glass.

Gabe whistled at him, held his ears forward and stuck out his tongue. Jude copied him. His mouth opened in a silent laugh; closed again. He pressed a palm against the glass, turned and slid down out of sight.

All Addie could see of Jude was a tuft of pale curled hair above the parcel shelf.

Flo appeared. She ran up to the car, her body held

low. Gabe whistled for her to come away, but she sat down beside it. Her tail swept slowly from side to side, whisking dust into the air. Sunni rushed forward and took hold of her collar.

'Come on, Flo,' she said. 'Out of the way then.' She stroked her head and led her over to stand beside Addie.

Addie couldn't watch Jude leave. She knelt down next to Flo. The dog panted; her breath hot on Addie's cheek. Her eyes searched Addie's.

'I know, girl,' Addie whispered. 'I know. You'll see Jude again soon.'

She really hoped that was true.

Flo licked Addie's neck; lifted one paw for her to hold.

'Bye,' Ruth called out. 'Bye, Jude.' She waved and blew a kiss.

The car engine leapt into life.

'Bye, lad,' Sam shouted. 'Bye for now.'

The purr of the engine. A toot of the horn.

The crunch and swish of tyres on dry cobbles.

And Jude was gone.

Widget appeared from nowhere, hurried across to where Addie was standing with Sam, Ruth, Gabe and Sunni. He weaved his warm body in and out of their legs, his tail held high and quivering. For once, he wasn't purring. He wandered back into the hallway.

'Right,' Gabe said, 'first one into the kitchen gets the biggest piece of cake.' He reached his arms towards Ruth. 'I'll carry it in for you, Ma.'

Sunni stepped in front of him. 'No way! I'll do it!' She took the box from Ruth, held it out in front of her, arms outstretched, and walked slowly, carefully, towards the house. Addie saw that she was trying not to cry.

Sam put an arm across Ruth's shoulders. He beckoned to Addie. 'Better get inside, Addie. Before it's too late. Jude will want to know what you thought of that cake.'

Addie nodded.

'School tomorrow,' Ruth said, as they walked into the hall, 'but then we'll have a special day out, all together, on Saturday. Lyme Regis. Where we went for Sunni's birthday, remember, Addie? Sam's arranged for the Jenkins boys to cover the farm. How does that sound, love?'

Addie glared at Ruth. A sharp, new pain jostled for space in her battered heart. It couldn't be soothed by sandcastles, fossils and seaside rock. Missing Jude couldn't be washed away, pulled out on the tide like the empty Coke cans and discarded feathers on the shoreline.

She turned away and strode into the kitchen.

Sunni was sitting at the table. On the chair with the green cushion.

'Get *off*,' Addie shouted. 'Get off Jude's chair!' She banged her fist down on the table next to Sunni. A pile of cake forks jumped into the air; clattered down again.

Sunni's bracelets clinked together. She burst into tears, covered her face with her hands. Addie's cheeks burned. Her head fizzed. It felt as if it might explode.

Ruth's arms folded round her, and round Sunni too; drew the girls close. She smelled like the lavender in the meadow. 'I know, girls,' she said. 'I know.' She ushered them forward. 'Gabe,' she said, 'three really big pieces of cake and some glasses of milk. In the snug, please. Soon as you can.'

She turned back just before they reached the door. 'And, remember: don't you give Flo any of that chocolate frosting no matter *how* sad she looks!'

THIRTY-ONE

Addie threw her schoolbag over the meadow gate and jumped down next to it. Birds chattered and sang all around her. Their pure, happy voices cut across other voices: school voices that buzzed around inside her head like wasps in a jar.

'How come you live with Sunni now?'

'Where's your mum, then?'

'Where's your dad?'

'Are your parents in prison? What did they do?'

'Are you an orphan?'

'Can't you talk?'

'Be like that then. Who cares?'

Addie's new school sat on a wide green, among white cottages, instead of graffiti-strewn concrete and kebab shops. But it was just the same as her old one.

No. It was worse.

At Gas Street School, back home, Addie was always alone. At Greenbank School, she wished she *could* be.

248

Why couldn't everyone just leave her be? She wasn't going to tell them *anything*. They wouldn't understand. Wouldn't want to be her friends.

And even if they did, Addie didn't care.

She was better off without any friends. They'd just dump her like Hattie had done.

She brushed at her eyes.

Jude had been her friend, though. Her *real* friend.

And somewhere, out on the moor, was her best friend of all. No one at Greenbank School would *ever* have a friend like him.

She squinted in the sunlight; trailed her hand in the grass as she walked. The blades had grown thick and long in the last few days of hot weather. But dandelions were taking over: a yellow and green invading army, blotting out the remains of Jude's spring garden.

Blotting out Jude.

A cluster of wispy dandelion clocks stood guard outside the entrance to his treehouse. Addie kicked at them, sending a cloud of tiny parachute troops into the air.

Why did things always have to change?

She crawled over the beheaded stalks; felt sap, wet and sticky, on her hands and knees. Jude would be cross with her, she knew. He loved all flowers, even weeds.

She pushed her head and shoulders in through the entrance to the treehouse. Dry, dusty air filled her nostrils. She caught sight of Jude's wobbly, hopeful words, picked out by a thin finger of sunlight.

Jude
and
thomas
Their place.

Thomas. Jude was going to see Thomas next month, Ruth said. Maybe his brother would come to live with him; would share the treehouse with the ladder and the red door.

Jude wouldn't need Addie for a friend if he got Thomas back.

Maybe the foal had a brother. Or a new friend.

A better friend than Addie.

Tears crawled down Addie's cheeks. She brushed them away.

She could visit Jude in the holidays. His new dads had promised. And they seemed like proper dads. The sort that kept promises.

The foal was back with his mam. Back home.

Where he *should* be.

Addie sat back on her heels. She wiped her sleeve across her face. She tried to feel happy for all of them.

It didn't work.

The tears kept coming; kept coming. Addie felt as if everything that made her brave was trickling out of her. As if she was dissolving; becoming part of the swirling dust, part of the emptiness of Jude's treehouse.

As if she was disappearing.

She crawled back out into the meadow. She sat down on a gnarled root, her wet chin in her hands, and waited for the tears to stop.

The sun slid low across the grass, as if reaching out for Addie. It was getting late. She'd been in the meadow longer than she thought. She should go indoors: Ruth would be wondering where she was.

But she couldn't go now. She felt paper-thin; as transparent as a wind-blown leaf. Everyone would be able to see right inside her.

A curled grey feather lifted in the breeze, drifted against Addie's leg: a soft, fledgling feather, no longer needed. Addie stared up into the waving branches above her head, saw the now abandoned nests just visible among the bright summer leaves. The young birds would return to the oak in spring, Gabe said. They would come home to build new families there, where their own lives had begun.

If only *she* was free like the half-grown birds. Free to soar above the moorland; to see the foal, safely at his mother's side. Free to fly to her brown brick house.

Free to fly home to Mam.

She turned, ran her hands over the trunk of the oak. It was warm, welcoming. She reached higher, tucked her fingers inside craters in the ancient bark, and wedged the toe of her right shoe inside another. She lifted her body from the ground. It felt light as air, as if her bones were hollow. As if she were a bird.

She glanced down, looked up, climbed on.

The leaves whispered to one another; stilled suddenly as Addie reached for a low branch. It wavered. It was too thin to take her weight. Her left foot twisted, dislodged some loose bark. Addie looked down again. She had climbed further from the ground than she had realised. She thought of the baby bird Jude had found under the tree, frail and broken, dislodged too soon from the safety of its nest.

What would happen if *she* was to fall?

She looked up again, saw thick branches spreading like strong arms to hold her. To hide her. She could do this. She tightened her grip and felt for another foothole.

Addie pressed herself tightly into the crook of a sturdy branch, her back against the trunk of the oak. Curtains of vivid leaves enclosed her, shielded her from view. She let her legs dangle among them.

To her left, the tops of the farmhouse chimneys were visible. Ruth would be in the kitchen now, preparing tea. Addie hoped she wouldn't start to worry; that she wouldn't come looking for her just yet.

She twisted round a little, looked over her right shoulder through the quivering leaves. She caught glimpses of other trees, pointed conifers, pushing into the sky beyond the meadow. If she climbed higher, might she be able to see the start of the moorland – might she see any of the ponies?

She swung one leg over the branch, straddled it for better balance, and searched for another strong branch. The next suitable one was perhaps four feet above her. Could she reach it? She wasn't sure. She shuffled back towards the trunk, felt for further places to get a grip. As she did so she remembered another tree.

Penny's tree. Printed in thick black lines on smooth white paper. A trickster-tree, waiting for Addie to spill her secrets in its bare branches . . .

'Imagine yourself sitting high in this tree,' Penny said. 'Who would you want with you in your tree? Where would they sit? Who would sit closest to you? Can you draw those people for me?'

Addie chose blue, brown and yellow pens. She drew herself and Mam on the topmost branch, pressed together: not a sliver of white sky-space between them. Mam was wearing her big blue hat. The one they chose together at a jumble sale in town.

Penny nodded; smiled. 'You love your mum,' she said. 'I wonder, now. Is there someone else? Someone on another branch? Someone on the ground, perhaps. Someone to catch you if you fall?'

Addie picked up a thick red pen. She wrote in careful letters underneath Penny's tree:

MAM WOULD NEVER LET ME FALL

Addie pressed her face against the rough surface of the tree trunk. She wrapped both arms round it, suddenly uncertain of her balance.

Her red pen told lies.

THIRTY-TWO

Addie squinted down through the foliage. The dandelions below blurred together like splashes of sunshine on the grass. It had been easy to climb this high. She hoped it would be as easy to get down when she wanted to.

Barking. Flo's bark.

The faint clunk of the meadow gate.

A whistle. Gabe's whistle.

'Addie?'

'Addie – you in the treehouse?'

His voice grew closer; louder. Addie heard Flo's rough, panting breaths. She glimpsed a flash of white-tipped tail.

'Addie? Don't make me send in the dogs . . . well, dog. I give you fair warning, she's been taught to lick her finds to death.'

Gabe's last few words were was muffled, as if he had stuck his head inside the tree.

Flo whined and yelped. Her feet scratched and scrabbled. Addie caught sight of her black and white head as she leapt at the tree trunk.

'Ah! Up there is she, Flo. Well done. Good girl. Now, wait!'

A pause. More scrabbling. Heavy breaths.

Gabe's wild red curls – beanie-free for once – appeared through the leaves beneath Addie's feet.

He grinned up at her and swung his way towards her, as easily as a squirrel.

'Shuffle along a bit then,' he said. 'Make room. Or are you not in the mood for visitors today?'

'I'm not shuffling anywhere,' Addie said. She wasn't moving further down the branch. It might not take Gabe's weight as well as hers.

'Like that is it?' Gabe twisted, stretched a leg to the side and disappeared round the back of the tree. Addie heard mutterings that Ruth would not have approved of; a heavy intake of breath. Gabe's legs swung down from above her head. His feet bicycled in the air, searching for a landing place.

'Now might be a good time to help,' Gabe said. 'If – it's – not – too much trouble.'

Addie grabbed one of his ankles and placed his foot

next to her on the branch. The other foot joined it. Gabe slithered to sit beside her, trailing one arm over her shoulder, a hand against the trunk for balance.

'You could have killed yourself, idiot!'

'Nah. Not me. Not with my circus ancestry and all.'

Addie stared at him.

'OK,' Gabe said, 'that one's a fib.' He brushed bits of bark from his hair, swept his fringe back and studied Addie's face. 'But I know this old tree like the back of my hand. It was *my* hiding place once.'

'I'm not hiding,' Addie said. 'I just like it up here.'

Gabe studied her face. His eyes grew greener than ever, as if he was part of the tree itself. 'This old oak knows all my secrets,' he said. 'But it has never told a soul. What comes out in the tree, stays in the tree. Oak-tree ethics or something.'

'You talked to a tree?'

'Used to. It helped. All this muddled stuff in my head, it got sorted somehow up here. I dunno: got smaller. Other times, it all just floated away in the air, like it was nothing really.' He grinned. 'But then, as you know, I'm weird.'

Addie smiled back. She hadn't known she was going to. 'Yep,' she said. 'You are.' She looked away, back towards the dark tops of the distant pines. She thought of the foal, how she had told *him* things. How he had listened and understood. The hollow spaces inside her filled with cold, heavy stones.

'Pretty impressive, you being up this high,' Gabe said. 'Sunni only got as far as . . .' he leaned forward, pointed to a short fat branch further down the tree. 'That one there.'

Addie shook her head. Sunni in a tree? No way. Never.

'Cross my heart,' Gabe said. 'Took some persuading. But, man, did she need to be up here when she first came to us. Think she might have spontaneously combusted without this tree. She might have been small, but *whoa* . . . was she big trouble.'

'Why?'

Gabe raised an eyebrow, as if Addie already knew the answer to her question. He pulled a packet of cherry sweets from his pocket, held it out to Addie. 'Sustenance for tree creatures,' he said.

Addie took one. She folded it inside her palm. It was sticky against her skin.

Gabe tucked a sweet inside his cheek 'Proper little spitfire, was our Sunni,' he said. 'Worse than Widget when Mum gets the brush and comb out.' He nodded at

Addie, that eyebrow raised again. 'Even worse than you. And the Sunni death stares? Major.'

Addie remembered Sunni, back there at Tarr Steps: remembered her fierceness. Her fear.

'I've seen it, the death stare,' she said.

Gabe nodded, smiled. 'Lucky to survive then.' He crunched, grinned again.

'So how come Sunni just stays here? You know, like you're her family now? She nearly killed me when she thought she might have to leave.'

'That's Sunni's story to tell, Addie,' Gabe said. 'You'll have to ask her.' His leaf-green eyes were on Addie's again. 'But maybe she learned a few things up here in the tree. Or maybe she learned them when she went back home for a bit, like she wanted back then.'

A pair of swallows appeared. They looped and swooped over the meadow, their forked tails streaming behind them like small banners. They looked happy, Addie thought; perfectly at home together in the endless sky. They dived down, sailed low against the ground. Gabe and Addie leaned forward, followed their easy glide.

Flo darted out across the grass. She ran in circles and barked as the birds sailed upwards again, far out of her reach.

'For a working sheepdog,' Gabe said, 'she's pretty daft.'

'Sunni reckons *she's* going to be a shepherd,' Addie said. 'With her own dog and everything.'

Gabe smiled. 'Reckon she might be, too. A sequined shepherd.' He crossed one leg over the other, closed his eyes. Like being half a mile up a tree with his feet dangling into space was nothing, was normal for him.

Like *he* could never fall.

'Reckon she'll be whatever she decides to be,' he said. He pointed at Addie, his eyes still shut. 'Same as you will.'

Could that be true? For her? Addie wished she could believe it. She watched leaf shadows play across Gabe's face, making him more a part of the tree than ever.

'That stuff in your head,' she said. 'When you used to hide up here ...'

Gabe opened his eyes.

'School stuff, mainly.'

'You don't go to school.'

'Used to. And will do again soon. Exams and all. He shrugged. 'Infants was great. I loved it. Juniors – well, that didn't work out so well. There were these kids. These three boys.'

'Bullying you?'

Gabe nodded.

'Why? What about?'

'Being adopted. Having red hair. Being me.' He shook his head. 'Anything. Turned out two of them had their own stuff going on. You know, difficult stuff at home. Good job I told, in the end. For them as well as me.'

Darren Oates' freckled face flashed in front of Addie. Became his dad's face: red and angry; his mam's face: blue shadows leaking through her thick orange make-up. Had Darren picked on Addie because he had been afraid too?

What about the kids at Greenbank with their constant questions – their wasp-sting words?

A shrill note split Addie's thoughts: rising, falling. Lifting through the trees.

'Did you hear that?' Addie craned her neck in the direction of the sound.

Gabe pulled his lips back in mock fear. 'The Beast of Exmoor!'

Addie shivered, suddenly back on the night-time moor. 'Funny,' she said.

Gabe's face was serious again. 'Sunni told me, Addie. About those kids.' He rested a hand on her arm. 'If they keep giving you a hard time, tell Ruth. OK? Or Sam.

They'll help. Like they helped Sunni. Before the wonders of BFF Mira!'

Addie looked away. Sunni. She should keep her nose out of Addie's business.

'Unless you can face the alternative, that is.'

Addie looked back at Gabe; sighed. 'What?'

He grinned. 'I wade in, pants over my trousers. Full Superman thing. I blast the enemy to oblivion.'

'Thanks, but no thanks,' Addie said. She felt the rise of tears again. Different tears, softer. Something warm washed over the cold stones inside her, swept words up through her throat and out into the air before she knew what was happening.

'At home,' she said, 'at my last school. There was this boy, Darren. Well, he was the worst.'

Gabe was still. The tree was still. Addie clenched her fist round Gabe's sweet, as if to crush it.

'I told Mam. She said she'd make it stop. She said she'd come into school and speak to my teacher.' Addie unfolded her hand, poked at the melting red stickiness there. 'So she did. The next day. At lunchbreak.'

Gabe waited.

'She – there was this big argument in the playground. Mam shouted at one of the teachers. It wasn't even *my* teacher. And she nearly fell over. Twice.'

The stones were cold again. One of them had lodged in Addie's throat.

'Everybody saw. Everybody knew . . .' Addie's breath was ragged. Like the stones were in her lungs now, too. She flicked the remains of the cherry sweet from her palm and steadied herself with both hands on the branch. 'Everything just got worse after that.'

Gabe put a hand on her shoulder.

'She promised,' Addie said. Her voice caught on a fragment of stone; cracked. 'She promised she wouldn't drink that day, but she did.'

Gabe pulled a leaf from the end of a thin twig. He twirled it in his fingers.

'You'd think it was simple, being a tree, wouldn't you?' he said.

Addie sighed. She watched the leaf spin back and forth. She didn't want to talk trees. Not now.

'You'd think: trees, they just *are*,' Gabe said. 'They just know how to be trees.'

'*What?*' Addie shook her head.

'But sometimes, things go wrong. Even for trees. Take Ma's apple trees, right: two years back, not a single apple on half of them. The next year, hundreds of 'em. Ma was making pies and chutney for weeks.' He looked up into the canopy of leaves above their heads. 'Except there was this one tree, it just sort of withered. Until Dad dug it up and planted it somewhere else. It still doesn't make many apples, but it's pretty, you know: a proper *tree*. After some help from Dad.'

'I don't see . . .'

'Being a person, right, that's a whole lot harder than being a tree.'

Addie stared at him. He was nuts.

Gabe looked straight into her eyes. 'It's just, maybe your mum chose the wrong kind of help to get *her* through, that's all.' He shrugged. 'Now she's getting the right kind. In the right place. She's brave. Like you are.' He let go of the leaf.

Addie watched Gabe's leaf drift from side to side. It floated softly to the ground. A small parachute. 'That's what Penny said,' she whispered.

Gabe nodded. '*She* knows things too then, doesn't she?'

He stretched, patted his stomach. 'We should go in,' he said. 'Dad's pizzas. You don't want to miss those. And anyway –' he wriggled – 'my bum's gone numb.' He shifted his position on the branch, readied himself to climb down.

The shrill sound came again. Closer this time. And louder. It rippled through Addie, echoed inside her bones.

She caught hold of Gabe's sleeve. 'Wait. Gabe. Help me stand up.'

'You don't need to stand to climb down. Best if you twist on to your stomach and feel with your feet for the next branch. I'll help you.'

Addie was already struggling to her feet, her arms reaching round the trunk. Could she see from here?

Her heart fluttered, lifted and jumped like a fledgling bird. That sound: she was right. She knew she was.

She strained to see through the mesh of leaves, stretched up on to her toes.

'Hey, steady on.' Gabe's hands were round her ankles. 'It's me that's the trapeze artist!'

Addie cupped a hand to her mouth. 'Wait! I'm coming!' she shouted. She looked back over her shoulder at Gabe, still hugging the tree. 'Show me the best way down. Quick!'

'Calm down first. I don't fancy getting Ma on my case when you end up with two broken legs.'

'It's him,' Addie said. 'Don't you get it? It's the foal. He's back.'

'Addie, I know you miss him, but it won't be –'

'If you're not going to help . . .' Addie slithered on to her stomach, legs dangling into nothingness.

'OK. OK. I'll go first. Follow me. And be *careful*!'

Addie's descent was more of a slide than a climb. Her hands and feet skidded over the bark, snatched briefly at each anchor point as Gabe moved on to the next. Her palms stung. There was a trickle of hot blood down her right wrist. Her knees throbbed under her jeans as they moved against the trunk of the oak. She didn't care.

She felt Gabe's eyes on her the whole time; heard his voice guiding her like a rope. But she had no idea what he was saying. Her ears strained above his words, above the sigh of leaves, the scratch of bark, the whine of the sheepdog beneath them.

'I'm here!' she yelled into the air. 'I'm coming.'

❄

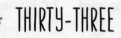

THIRTY-THREE

Addie's legs thrashed through the thick field grass behind the meadow; through the golden buttercups and clusters of purple clover. Nettles brushed across her hands. She barely felt their sting.

'Addie! Slow down a minute . . .'

Gabe was catching up with her. She'd made him stay back and tether Flo, so she couldn't race on ahead and spook the foal.

'Do you even know where you're heading?' His words came staccato. He was out of breath already.

Addie looked back over her shoulder. 'Yes. But don't *shout*.'

An invisible thread pulled Addie onwards, over a stile and into the second field. Sheep scattered as she and Gabe appeared. Half-grown lambs bleated and skittered towards the protection of the flock.

'Go careful!' Gabe drew level with her. 'Don't upset them.'

Addie slowed slightly.

She pointed to a ragged line of conifers, just beyond the fence at the bottom of the field. 'There,' she said. She ran on. Her eyes scanned the fence for the best place to climb over. She couldn't waste time searching for the gate.

Gabe caught at her sleeve. 'No, Addie. That's electric fencing. To keep the foxes out and the sheep in. The wires run behind the wooden slats. You can't climb over it.'

Addie's heart was loud in her ears. With it, another, remembered, beat. She stood still.

'Shhh! Listen!'

Twigs snapped. She heard the soft thud, thump, thud of hooves on the matted ground beneath the trees. A snorted breath.

'I'm here. It's me!' Addie lunged forward.

Gabe gripped her arm. 'No!' he said. 'Don't. I'll lift you, all right? I'll lift you clear of the fence.'

Addie looked at him for a moment; nodded. 'Quick, then. Quick.'

Gabe scooped her up, one arm round her back, the other under her knees. 'I'm aiming for that mossy bit there,' he said. 'Landing technique's down to you.' He heaved her high against his chest, held her above the fence for a second and then she was on her bottom on the other side. Nowhere near the mossy bit.

'You OK?' Gabe grinned his lopsided grin. 'I'm useless at throwing.'

Addie stood up, brushed bracken and bits of bark from her hands. 'Thanks,' she said. 'For telling me.'

She took a step closer to the trees. Another step.

The crackle of twigs; the thump of hooves again. Louder, closer now, blending with the thump of Addie's heart.

A pale muzzle pushed through the branches to Addie's right. Black, almond eyes peered out beneath a heavy fringe of mane. Between them, a white shape – a snowflake shape – clear and bright in the dappled light beneath the trees.

Addie stared. The foal stared back.

He lifted his head and whinnied softly. He emerged from the trees, his eyes locked on Addie's as he walked slowly towards her.

Addie stretched out a hand. The foal pushed his nose against it; came closer, nuzzled her face. He leaned in, rested his head on her shoulder. Addie wrapped her arms round his neck. She breathed him in.

He smelled different: of dust and earth and

forest pine; of something bitter and stale.

He felt different. Bonier. Taller. His coat was rough and tight against his body.

But he was the same.

Addie entwined her fingers in his mane, closed her eyes. 'You came back,' she whispered. 'You came back.' She felt her breathing slow and slip into a shared rhythm with the foal.

The foal lifted his head. His ears pricked and swivelled.

Gabe appeared behind them, his face almost as red as his hair.

'That gate's bloomin' miles away.' He pushed damp locks of hair from his forehead.

'Blimey,' he said. He nodded towards the foal.

'Told you,' Addie said.

The foal turned away from Gabe. He nudged at Addie's pocket with his nose.

'Haven't got anything for you in there this time,' Addie said. She reached round, patted his side. 'Hungry, are you?' She turned to Gabe. 'He's really thin.'

Gabe moved towards the foal. He backed away, looked at Addie for reassurance.

'It's OK,' Addie said. 'You know Gabe.'

A fly buzzed around the foal's eyes. He blinked his long lashes. Addie wafted it away with her hand.

Gabe smoothed his hand along the foal's back. 'His spine's a bit prominent.' He stopped. 'Ah. Had some trouble, have you, little guy?'

'What? Let me see.' Addie leaned round. She winced. There was a jagged wound on the foal's right flank, its edges black with dried blood. Damp, red flesh was visible between them. It looked very sore. Addie felt the sting of it on her own skin.

The foal flicked his tail, swung his head round and nudged Gabe away.

'He's not going to touch it,' Addie said. 'Don't worry.'

'Looks a bit like a bite,' Gabe said. 'Or he might have snagged himself on something, I suppose. Either way, that wound needs cleaning up.'

'Let's go then. Get him home – I mean, back to the farm,' Addie said.

Gabe scratched his head. 'If he'll come with us. We haven't got a rope or anything to lead him with.'

'He'll follow me. Which way's the gate?'

Gabe pointed to the right. 'Let's try it then; see if he'll come. But he's been back in the wild for a couple of months now, Addie. He'll have changed.'

Addie ignored him. She made a clicking sound through her teeth. The foal blew down his nose and stepped forward.

He walked slowly at Addie's side, more slowly still by the time the tall farmhouse chimneys came into view beyond the meadow. His skin glistened with sweat. He kept stopping. Addie thought of him gambolling in the grass with her and Jude, agile as a spring lamb – rolling on his back, kicking his legs in the air for the sheer joy of being alive. Now, he was moving like one of Sam's lumbering, reluctant cows. She touched Gabe's arm.

'He doesn't look right,' she said. 'D'you think he's just tired? Or really hungry?'

Gabe stooped, snatched up a blade of grass and chewed on it.

'He's tired, for sure. He must've been walking for ages before we found him. But there's no shortage of food for him along the way, Addie. I reckon it's more than that.' He placed a hand on the foal's neck. 'He's hotter than he should be now.'

Addie took the foal's face between her palms, pressed her forehead against his. Gabe was right. He was way too warm. 'Don't worry,' she said. 'You have a rest for a bit.'

'He can't walk any further,' she whispered to Gabe, Gabe shook his head. 'No. And I reckon he needs a drink, sharpish.'

Addie looked around her. Grass, bracken, trees: tinder-dry in the warmth of early summer. Only the grass to offer the foal any moisture at all. That wouldn't be enough. He needed fresh water.

'Ring Sam,' Addie said. 'Tell him to bring his truck – as close as he can get it, anyway.'

Gabe took his phone from his pocket, held it up; stepped from side to side. 'No signal, as per. Mind you, if there was, there'd be a hundred calls from Dad about tea being on the table.'

'You'll have to run back to the farm and get Sam then. I'll wait here.'

Gabe checked his phone again; stuffed it back into his pocket.

'I'll go and get Dad,' he said. 'But there's no way we'll get your foal in the truck. He's been in it before: that night we found him. He was terrified: fought like a little tiger, weak as he was. And he hasn't forgotten. Remember what happened with the pony people's jeep?'

Addie did remember. 'That was different,' she said. 'They were trying to take him away; maybe to sell him to strangers. She felt the foal shiver against her leg. 'Just go, OK? *Hurry up.*'

As soon as Gabe had left, the foal sank to the floor. He flopped on to one side, long legs stretched out. His stomach rose and fell sharply as he breathed. Addie sat down by his head and spoke softly into his ear.

'You'll be all right,' she said. 'You'll be at the farm soon.'

She pulled some long blades of fresh grass, put them by the foal's mouth. He licked at them briefly with his long tongue; blinked at Addie.

'That's OK,' Addie said. 'Don't worry.'

Addie curled up beside him, her face level with his. He stared into her eyes for a long moment. His heavy eyelids slid down.

Was he just sleeping?

Addie drew a piece of grass across his muzzle. Nothing. No twitch of his nostrils. She pressed her head against his side, listened for his heart above the beat of her own, loud in her ears.

It was there.

It was.

But it was faster than usual. What did that mean?

She rested her hand on his neck, felt the warmth of the evening sun on her skin, the damp heat of the foal's body on her palm. She should move him back into the shade of the trees. But there was no way she could do that by herself.

She sat up, strained to hear the sound of Sam's truck. There was nothing but the birds gossiping in the trees. It was way too soon. Gabe wouldn't even have reached the farm yet. The cackling laughter of crows rose from a nearby beech.

'Shut up, stupid crows!' Addie whispered through her teeth. 'Just shut up.' She wrapped her arms round her knees; hugged them tightly under her chin.

It would be OK, she told herself.

Sam would know what to do.

Please let him get here soon.

THIRTY-FOUR

The foal heard the truck before Addie did. He stirred and managed to struggle to his feet.

That was a good sign, Addie thought. Even though his legs wobbled and shook like they had done when he first came to the farm, and his breathing seemed faster than ever.

Panicked wingbeats sounded above as the rumble of the engine drew closer, louder. When it died away, the trees fell silent.

Sam and Gabe's voices sounded in the still air.

'Over here!' Addie called. She stroked the foal's nose, spoke gently to him. It couldn't be good for him to be upset just now. He settled a little; pushed his head under Addie's arm, as if to hide. He was shivering again. Tiny vibrations ran through Addie's body as he pressed himself close. He didn't move when Sam appeared, carrying a metal bucket and a green towel.

Sam approached slowly, kept his voice low and soft.

He smiled at Addie. 'Gabe's waiting with Flo in the truck. You OK, sweetheart?'

'I'm fine,' Addie said. 'But something's really wrong with the foal. You can help him, can't you? Please, Sam.'

Sam glanced at the wound on the foal's flank. He felt the pulse in his neck. His eyes crinkled in concern. 'Well now, youngster,' he said. 'You've come a long way to find your friend, haven't you?' He put the bucket down next to him. 'Let's see if you'll take a drink.'

The foal sniffed at the bucket. Addie bent down, dipped her fingers in the water and swirled the surface. 'Come on,' she said. 'It'll make you feel better.'

The foal blinked at Addie, pushed his nose deep into the bucket. His long tongue curled close to Addie's fingers as he scooped the cool water into his mouth.

'Well done,' Addie whispered. 'Good boy.' She looked up at Sam.

'It's my fault he's hurt and sick, isn't it?' she said. She chewed at her lip. 'I thought he wanted to go home and be with his mam. I thought he'd be happy. And safe.'

Sam held her gaze. 'It's no one's fault, Addie.' He ruffled her hair. 'You did what you thought was best for him. But right now, this little guy's made it pretty clear that it didn't work out. He needs your help and that's

278

why he's back. Some spirit he's got; coming all that way by himself.'

The foal lifted his head and shook it from side to side, sending crystal droplets into the air. He stood a little taller; flicked his tail.

'The water's perked him up a bit, anyway. But we'd best get him back quickly. I've called the vet out.' Sam picked up the bucket. 'Let's see if he'll walk again now. We can take it slowly.'

Sam handed her the towel. 'Give him a gentle rub down with this. His skin's damp. We don't want him getting chilled on the way. Sun's going down.'

'But the truck,' Addie said. 'Gabe said he'll be too scared. Like before.'

Sam glanced at the foal, whose eyes were fixed on Addie.

'*You'll* be in that truck this time,' he said. 'He'll be absolutely fine.'

Sam was right.

The foal lay quietly in the back of the truck all the way to the farm, his head in Addie's lap, heavy and hot.

He needed ten stitches. Addie held his face and spoke softly to him as Jo, the vet, did her sewing, then gave him an injection. The foal's eyes never left Addie's face until Jo moved away and snapped her bag shut.

Sam showed Addie how to mix some thin, nutritious porridge meal. The foal didn't finish it all, but he did take another long drink of water. Jo said that was the most important thing for now. That and a good rest.

Addie made him a bed of fresh straw and covered him with a light blanket. When Sam went off to shut the pigs and chickens in their pens for the night, she gathered up some more straw and curled up on it alongside him. She wasn't letting him out of her sight.

Ruth appeared in the barn doorway, torch in hand. She was wearing Sam's dressing gown and her green wellies. 'Thought so,' she said. There was a smile in her voice.

She knelt down next to Addie on the straw.

'Peas in a pod, you two,' she said. She tilted her head towards the foal. 'Both as brave and determined as can be.'

Addie looked away; watched shadows play in the torchlight. 'Jo thinks the other ponies picked on him,' she said. 'When he went back.' She turned, looked into Ruth's face. 'His mam didn't keep him safe.'

Ruth pushed a stray lock of curls away from Addie's eyes. 'Maybe she wasn't there, Addie. We just don't know. But something went wrong back there in the winter, didn't it? When he was left all alone in the snow?' She smiled her gentle smile. 'He's safe now, that's the thing. I'm just glad he knew where to come.'

She eased herself up to stand, one hand on her back, as if it was stiff.

'Come on, young lady,' she said. Your foal will be fine until morning now. Sam'll look in on him when he goes off to milk first thing, and he'll give him more medicine.' She held out her hand. 'You need your rest now, just like your friend does. You've both had quite a day!'

Addie opened her mouth to protest. Ruth smiled her 'no argument' smile. Even in the shifting light from her torch, it didn't waver.

THIRTY-FIVE

The kitchen windows were still open. A soft breeze lifted the small hairs on Addie's arms as she washed dust and dirt from her hands. A crane fly danced up and down the curtains near the sink, desperate to escape. Addie leaned in, shook it free of the fabric and watched it disappear into the night.

'As the foal's on the mend,' Ruth said, 'let's you and I have chat about school tomorrow. We can agree a plan to make things better.'

Addie looked down. She wasn't sure.

'For a start,' Ruth said, 'those new classmates of yours need to know that they've got a pony whisperer in their midst. One with wild adventures to share!'

Addie smiled a small smile. Maybe. Ruth knew things, after all.

Her stomach growled. 'Is there any of Sam's pizza left?' she asked.

Ruth nodded. 'In the Aga, keeping warm for you.'

She laughed, standing up to go and fetch it. 'You're lucky Gabe didn't realise!'

The pizza was delicious, loaded with ham and pineapple and crisp round the edges. Nearly as good as the one Mam used to make.

First Mam. Before.

Addie ate everything, ignored Gabe's – and Flo's – pleading eyes.

Sunni drained a glass of milk, pushed it aside and wiped her mouth with the back of her hand. She pointed at Gabe with a half-eaten apple. 'At least Flo's got a good excuse for being greedy,' she said. 'Unlike some people.'

Ruth laughed. She came and sat beside Addie, her hands cupped round a striped mug of tea. 'She does,' she said. 'But pizza is definitely *not* what she needs!'

Gabe scooped crumbs from Addie's plate, dropped them into his mouth. 'Go on then, Sunni, tell Addie *your* news. We know you're bursting.'

Sunni pushed her curtain of hair behind one ear, sat up importantly in her chair. Her black-brown eyes sparkled as brightly as her bracelets. 'Flo's having babies,' she announced. 'In August. And I'm keeping one. To train as a sheepdog.' She looked at Gabe. 'Aren't I?'

Gabe flung himself into the rocking chair. 'If you behave,' he said. 'And if you give me your share of any cake that Ma makes between now and when the pups arrive.'

'Babies? Really?' Addie looked at Flo, curled in her basket. She tried to picture the tiny beginnings of life tucked inside her feathered white belly. Would Flo know how to be a mother? Or would she need help, like some of Sam's ewes?

Like Mam.

Flo's tail thumped up and down. Her pink tongue lolled from her mouth. Addie was sure she was smiling.

'Clever dog,' she said. 'Good dog, Flo.'

Sunni was staring at Addie. 'You've got something in your hair,' she said.

'So?'

Sunni kept on staring. 'I'm glad the foal came back to stay,' she said. She reached over and pulled a short piece of straw from Addie's fringe.

Addie stared back at her. Sunni didn't even like the foal.

Sunni twisted the piece of straw in her fingers. 'I'm glad cos then he's just like me.'

'Yeah,' Gabe said. 'A whole heap of trouble.'

Addie smiled. 'He *can* stay, can't he, Ruth?' she said, suddenly anxious all over again.

Ruth glanced over at Gabe. He nodded back, whistled for Flo. 'C'mon, Sunni,' he said. 'You can help me and Flo check on the lambs. You need to get some practice in.'

Addie searched Ruth's face. What was going on?

Ruth rested her hand on Addie's arm. 'Sam wants to talk to you, Addie,' she said. 'We both do.' Her eyes were softer than ever; her voice gentle. 'We had a chat with the vet, before she left. She's concerned about that little foal. He's been through such a lot in his short life.'

Addie let the pizza fall back on to her plate. 'I know that,' she said. 'That's why it's good he came back here. I'm his friend. I'll look after him.'

Ruth nodded. 'And he couldn't *have* a better friend than you, Addie. He knows that; knows that you love him. He trusts you.'

Addie kept her eyes fixed on Ruth's face. 'So, that means –'

'That means you have to do your very best for him, Addie. Like you've always tried to do. But right now, that means thinking very hard about what this foal really needs for the future.'

Heat crept into Addie's face and burned behind her eyes. She looked away, fiddled with her fork. She knew *exactly* what this meant. It meant grown-ups deciding *they* knew best, deciding things the foal might not like. Things *she* might not like.

Well, she was the one who knew best about him. Not the vet who'd only met him three or four times, not Ruth and not Sam. He was 'just a sheep and cow man.'

'I already know what the foal needs,' she said. 'He needs *me*.'

Her bottom lip began to tremble. Images of the foal wandering wounded and alone on the moor pushed their way into her mind. She shouldn't have taken him back there.

She hadn't known best about that, had she? Not at all.

She covered her mouth with her hand. A large tear made its way down her cheek, slipped between her fingers.

Ruth drew her chair closer, put her arm round Addie's shoulders.

'You're right, Addie. The foal *does* need you. And you need him too. We can all see that. What we have to do is make a plan that lets you two be together as much as possible, but in a way that gives the foal the other things he needs, too: space to run free, the company of other ponies and people who really know about horses to watch over him. We can't give him those things here.' She leaned round, looked into Addie's face. 'And, Addie,' she said gently, 'the foal won't always have you here to look after him either, will he? What happens when you go home?'

Addie took in a shaky breath. 'Suppose,' she whispered. 'But that's not yet, is it?' And if he goes to that sanctuary, we'll hardly *ever* get to see each other while I *am* here. She wiped her hand over her eyes. 'It's *too far away*.'

Ruth shook her head. 'It doesn't need to be the sanctuary. Jo's given us some other ideas. Sam's already on the phone about one of them.'

Addie's heart fluttered and jumped in her chest. 'He's not – he can't make the foal go anywhere yet. He's sick!'

'It's all right, Addie. No. Not for a while. The foal needs some rest and recovery time. Sam's just checking out possibilities, that's all. All right?'

Addie nodded. Her head felt heavy on her shoulders.

'He's talking to Bill and Anne Johnson,' Ruth went on. 'Apparently, they're about to adopt a couple of Exmoor colts. It was all arranged through a special

Exmoor Pony Trust. Sam'll tell you all about it. *And –*' she paused, brought her hands together – 'Jo thinks that Anne and Bill might be open to taking your foal too. If she's right, it could be perfect. They certainly have the space and they really love their horses.'

Addie felt a quiver of hope. The Johnsons' farm was just down the road. She passed it every day on the way to school. If she cut across Jude's meadow, and round the edges of the Sam's cornfields, she could get there even quicker than that. She chewed at the inside of her cheek.

Could this be OK?

She thought of the horses that already lived at the Johnsons' farm. Peanut and Beauty: great, placid cobs with huge fluffy feet; Tulip and Lupin: the retired donkeys who stood patiently in the meadow, flicking their tails against the flies and waiting for Mrs Johnson to come and feed them apples. All were lovely, sweet creatures. They would be kind to her foal, she was sure.

But what about the new colts that were about to arrive?

'What if those new ponies don't like the foal?' she asked. 'What if they bully him?'

'Don't look so worried, Addie,' Ruth said. 'According

to Jo, the new colts are absolutely lovely – they're pretty tame, like your foal, and a little older – more mature. If it turns out that your little one might join them, Bill and Anne will do some careful introductions. They know about horses. And –' Ruth smiled her soft smile – 'they'd have *you* to help them, wouldn't they?'

Addie pushed back her chair. 'Can we go and find Sam?' she said. 'And see if the Johnsons said yes?'

Ruth got to her feet and pulled off her apron. 'Let's do that,' she said. 'He'll be in the snug. Nothing's certain yet, mind, Addie. We might have to think about a different plan.' She touched a finger to Addie's chin, lifted it a little; looked into her eyes. 'But, whatever happens, Addie, when things need to be decided, we'll decide them *together*. That's a promise.'

Addie woke with the birds. A bubble of excitement bounced in her chest. She sprang out of bed as soon as she heard footfalls on the landing, the thud of the front door.

She dressed and ran downstairs. The kettle whistled as she passed the kitchen. Gabe was in there, humming one of his silly tunes. Something sizzled in a pan: bacon. It smelled good.

But breakfast could wait. Mrs Johnson would have fresh-baked bread waiting. And thick golden honey from her own bees.

The front door was open. Early sunlight stretched into the hall.

Addie knelt down on the step and laced her trainers. The air was heavy with the scent of autumn roses. They seemed to have bloomed overnight, creamy pink against the red and yellow honeysuckle on the trellis round the door.

There was still a slight breeze, but it was going to be quite warm: another of Ruth's 'Indian summer' days. Addie would be fine in her thin T-shirt. She threw her sweatshirt on to the settle and set off across the yard.

Ruth came round the corner of the house. She was carrying a basket of eggs.

'I knew you'd be up with the larks again,' she said. She smiled, pointed to the basket. 'I'm going to do some hard-boiled eggs. For a picnic lunch. I thought we'd spend the morning on the beach; make the most of this surprising weather.'

Addie touched one of the eggs. It was still warm. She looked up at Ruth, shielding her eyes with her hand. 'I'm going over to the Johnsons' farm, though,' she said. 'You promised I could spend the whole day there, seeing as it's nearly the end of the holidays.'

Ruth laughed. 'I *know*,' she said. 'All sorted. Sam's staying behind. He has loads to do. But he'll check in on you every so often; bring you your lunch. Mira's coming with us to the beach, to keep Sunni company. And we'll have Gabe, so none of my picnic bakes will go to waste anyway!'

Addie laughed too. It felt strange. But familiar. Nice.

'Before you go, there's something for you, Addie. It

came yesterday.' Ruth fished inside the back pocket of her jeans. She brought out a blue envelope. Addie's name was on the front.

In Mam's lovely, looped writing.

'She promised she'd write,' Ruth said. 'Didn't she?'

Addie stared at the envelope. It was open.

'Someone's read it,' she said.

Ruth nodded. 'I did,' she said. And so did Penny. She sent it on for you from her office.' Her eyes were soft. 'It's your letter, I know, sweetheart. But Penny and I need to know what your mum's saying. Until she's fully on the mend.'

There was a single sheet of paper inside the envelope. Addie pulled it free. It fluttered in the breeze, like the wings of a blue butterfly. Like it might float away at any moment. Addie held on to it with both hands. She looked down at the cobbles, scuffed at them with the toe of her trainer.

'Do you think she *will* be one day? Mended? Back to how she was before?'

'I don't know, Addie. But I hope so,' Ruth said. 'In time. She seems to be doing much better now. You'll see, in your letter.' She smoothed Addie's hair. 'Would you like me to stay with you while you read it?'

Addie shook her head. 'It's OK. I'll read it later.'

'Well, I'm here if you need me then.' Ruth brushed a stray curl from Addie's face and tucked it behind her ear. 'And Sam will be around, remember? Just let Mrs Johnson know if you need him. If you need anything at all.'

Addie folded the letter; folded it again, so that it fitted inside her palm. 'Ruth,' she said, 'if I wanted to, could I stay here until Mam's *really* better? Even if that takes quite a long time?' She chewed at her bottom lip. 'And then I could see her sometimes. You know, like Sunni does.'

Ruth put down her basket. She closed her hands round Addie's; round Mam's thin blue letter. 'You can stay here as long as it takes, Addie. Penny and I have agreed that with David. You remember David, from our last meeting?'

Addie nodded. The owl man. She had liked his sing-song voice.

'And whatever happens, Addie,' Ruth said, 'you're part of this family now, for as long as you want to be. So when you do go home to that brown brick house of yours, you can still come and see us. You can come and stay for weekends, or holidays, if your mum agrees. It'll give her a bit of time to herself. Mums need that sometimes.'

Addie studied Ruth's face. She nodded. 'I'll have to come back a lot,' she said. 'Or the foal will miss me too much.'

'Good!' Ruth said. 'I'm glad. Now, young lady, if you hang on just a minute, Sam will drop you over at the Johnsons' place.'

Right on cue, Sam's blue truck rumbled into the yard. Sam waved through the window. 'Taxi for Miss Jones,' he called.

As Addie climbed in beside him. He handed her a package wrapped in brown paper.

'Bacon sandwich,' he said. 'Compliments of the chef.'

The foal was watching for her over his stable door. Addie put her arms round his neck, hugged him close. 'Breakfast first,' she said, 'then a bit later, you're going out to play.'

The foal nuzzled her face, snorted softly. She ran her hands over his smooth back and felt for the faint silver scar on his flank. It was barely there at all now. 'Looking good,' she said. 'Beautiful boy.'

She checked he had water and filled his feed bucket, put it down under his nose.

'There you go,' she said. 'Don't eat it too quickly, though.'

She slid down on to the straw and unfolded the blue letter. 'It's from my mam,' she told the foal.

He lifted his head from the bucket. His ears twitched; swivelled from side to side.

He was listening. Like he always did.

Addie squinted at Mam's beautiful looped words. 'She's coming to see me,' she said. 'After I start back at school. Penny's bringing her.' She looked into the foal's face. 'She says she's painting me a picture.'

The foal's eyes glistened. He blinked twice, went back to the last of his meal.

Addie wiped at her own eyes, folded the letter; smoothed the creases to make it flat. She put it in her back pocket. She stroked the foal's nose. 'When Mam comes,' she said, 'I'll ask her to paint a picture of you too.'

The foal whinnied softly. He lowered himself on to the straw. Addie rested her head on his neck, felt the beat of blood through his veins: strong now; steady. She curled her body into his.

Morning sunshine crept into the stable, warm and kind. It wrapped itself round Addie and the foal. They dozed, fell into a sound sleep. Neither stirred when Mrs Johnson came to check on them. Neither heard Sam put a picnic basket on the straw beside them and tiptoe away in his heavy boots.

It was Sunni who woke them: her quick feet on the stone floor, the impatient jangle of her bracelets; her high, excited voice.

Addie yawned and stretched. She felt as if she had slept for years.

Sunni thrust her hand under Addie's nose. Her skin smelled of salt.

'Brought you something from the beach,' she said.

Addie blinked. Focused.

It was a curled shell: pink and white and perfect.

'It's still got the sea inside it.' Sunni folded her arms. 'I checked.'

Addie lifted the shell to her ear. She smiled.

'Thanks, Sunni,' she said. 'That's brilliant. I'll keep it to give to Mam.'

She kissed the foal's forehead. 'Up you get, sleepy-head,' she said. 'Time to go and see your new friends again.' She brushed straw from her jeans and looped the picnic basket over one arm. 'Come on, Sunni,' she said. 'If you like, we can share.'

The colts, Ziggy and Stardust, stood grazing in the far corner of the paddock. They lifted their dark heads and called to the foal. He whinnied in reply; kicked out his hind legs, skipped and skittered towards them across the dew-soaked grass. Addie and Sunni laughed as they watched him dance.

If only Jude could see him now, Addie thought. Very soon, he would.

A burnt-orange leaf drifted past her face. She looked up at the new September sky. A flock of birds flew overhead, on their way to warmer climes. But any day now, Flo's autumn babies would arrive.

Before long, it would be winter again at Oaktree Farm.

Addie hoped there would be snow. Deep, glistening *Exmoor* snow.

Snow for building things.

ACKNOWLEDGEMENTS

Goodness, where do I begin? So many people have helped clear a way through the wilderness for Addie and her snow foal; helped them to find their home.

First mention goes to the children and families in whose real stories I played a small part, just for a moment, as a social worker. It was an immense privilege. Thank you for all that you taught me.

My special thanks to my 'super-agent', Emily Talbot, for her professional energy, her commitment and warm support whenever needed; to my lovely editor, Lindsey Heaven, for listening to Addie, Jude, Sunni, and Gabe; for understanding what they were trying to say. For listening to me, then helping me to hear what was best for this book. To everyone else at Egmont UK, notably Ali Dougal, Lucy Courtenay, and the Design team for their enthusiasm and sympathetic handling of my work. Illustrator Keith Robinson must have particular mention for the stunning cover. It is perfection.

My gratitude and respect to the wonderful staff of Bath Spa University, including Paul Meyer, who believed in me and inspired me from the start, the creative force that is Joanna Nadin, and my wonderful tutors on the MA Writing for Young People: David Almond, Julia Green, Steve Voake and Janine Amos. Thank you for your wise guidance and expertise; for the challenges, the opportunities, and the support. And as for my fabulous MA peers, especially the 'Aubergines' – what can I say? Only that I couldn't have done it without you . . .

Thank you to those true friends who offered me a listening ear, or helped keep a roof over my head and the Exmoor Beast from my door, among them: Fi and Giles Williams, Lucy Cuthew, 'the two Nicks', Chris Milford and Richard Taylor. There are others. I will never forget any of you.

Above all else, heartfelt thanks to my family. To my late mother, Jean Hutchinson, for everything she was and all that she gave me. Her creativity and gentle spirit glitter from these pages. To my astonishing children, Ali, Joe, Josh, Emma and Oli; their very special partners Kristen, Emily, Lyndy, Ash and Phoebe, and my beautiful grandsons, Luca and Jules: thank you for the inspiration and encouragement, the technical advice, the ridiculous gifs, the laughter and the love. You are everywhere in this book and everything that matters most in my world. My endless summer-blue sky.

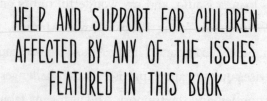

HELP AND SUPPORT FOR CHILDREN AFFECTED BY ANY OF THE ISSUES FEATURED IN THIS BOOK

- Childline: www.childline.org.uk 0800 1111
- Nacoa: The National Association for Children of Alcoholics: www.nacoa.org.uk/children.html 0800 358 3456
- NSPCC: www.nspcc.org.uk
- CoramBAAF Fostering and Adoption Agency: www.coramvoice.org.uk/contact-us (The 'Always Heard' helpline for young people: www.coram. org.uk/how-we-do-it/coram-voice-getting-young-voices-heard 0808 800 5792)
- Farms for City Children (Michael Morpurgo): www.farmsforcitychildren.org

For interest/education/conservation support:
- The Exmoor Pony Centre: www.moorlandmousietrust.org.uk
- The Exmoor Pony Society: www.exmoorponysociety.org.uk